Bison Frontiers of Imagination

THE SAVAGE GENTLEMAN

Philip Wylie

Introduction to the Bison Books edition by

Richard A. Lupoff

University of Nebraska Press
Lincoln and London

First Nebraska paperback printing: 2010

Library of Congress Cataloging-in-Publication Data

Wylie, Philip, 1902-1971.
The savage gentleman / Philip Wylie; introduction
to the Bison Books edition by Richard A. Lupoff.
p. cm. — (Bison frontiers of imagination)
ISBN 978-0-8032-3460-4 (pbk.: alk. paper)
1. Boys — Fiction. 2. Fathers and sons — Fiction.
3. Islands — Fiction. 4. Young men — Fiction.
5. Alienation (Social psychology) — Fiction.
6. Misogyny — Fiction. I. Title.
PS3545.Y46S38   2010
813'.52 — dc22
2010025228

Set in Constantia by Kim Essman.
Designed by Helena Esnerova.

INTRODUCTION

Richard A. Lupoff

In the twenty-first century, Philip Wylie is not exactly a household name, but sixty-odd years ago Wylie was a famous — and controversial — figure. This notoriety was the product of *Generation of Vipers* (1942), a scathing critique of American society as Wylie then saw it. His chief target was the phenomenon that he called "momism."

The conclusion that he drew was that the population coming of age in this country were unworthy of the heritage created by their more industrious and committed forebears. Ironically, the generation that Wylie castigated would become known, in later decades, as "the greatest generation." As for "momism," Wylie's railing against womankind was a theme that informed many of his works, including *The Savage Gentleman*.

Philip Gordon Wylie was born May 12, 1902, in Beverly, Massachusetts. His father was a Presbyterian minister. His mother was a writer of some note, who died when Philip was five. The elder Wylie remarried, but apparently Philip did not get along well with either his father or his stepmother. He grew up in New Jersey and Ohio and attended Princeton University but did not receive a degree. He was married twice, his first marriage ending in divorce. These misfortunes — the early death of Wylie's mother, his unhappy relationship with his stepmother, and the failure of his first marriage — in all likelihood contributed to his ongoing uneasiness when it came to women.

He began writing for publication while still a student. By 1925, having moved to New York, he was one of the original editors of the *New Yorker* and a full-fledged member of the Algonquin Round Table. By 1927 he had managed to get himself fired from the *New Yorker*; instead of seeking another editorial berth, he started selling fiction. At first he had success in the pulp field, selling to many magazines, including *Black Mask*, *Blue Book*, *Detective Story Magazine*, *Fantastic*, *Five Detective Novels*, *Live Girl Stories*, *Mystery*, *Triple Detective*, *Worlds Beyond*, and *Zest*. In time he graduated to the slicks, where pay rates were higher, the readership was larger, and the prestige was greater. His output was both varied and prolific. His series about the charter-boat operators Crunch and Des alone ran to more than one hundred stories in the *Saturday Evening Post*.

He was always intrigued by science fiction. In a 1953 essay titled "Science Fiction and Sanity in an Age of Crisis," he mentions his boyhood fondness for pulp science fiction. However, by this time, while still producing science fiction of his own, he had largely turned against his colleagues in the field. He writes that "their orientation leads most frequently to wild adventure, wanton genocide on alien planets, gigantic destruction and a piddling phantasmagoria of impossible nonsense." He concludes, "Most science fiction is trash, ill-conceived and badly written." Oddly, the only works he mentions specifically are Olaf Stapledon's *Odd John*, H. G. Wells's *The Shape of Things to Come*, and the film *The Day the Earth Stood Still*, based on the short story "Farewell to the Master" by Harry Bates.

Wylie's own science fiction was not only successful in its own right, but is believed by many scholars and critics of mass culture to have heavily influenced Wylie's contemporaries in the pulp field and in the world of comic books, as well.

Gladiator (1930) is the story of a superman created in a laboratory experiment. The superman is "created" by his father through prenatal chemical infusions, delivered through his mother. The development of such a superman (lowercase "s") anticipates the origin story of the comic-book hero Captain America and also that of the Human Torch. And of course, as an instance of life imitating art, the steroid scandals of the 1990s and 2000s in the world of professional sports could well have been based on Wylie's novel.

When Worlds Collide (1933), cowritten with Wylie's sometime editor Edwin Balmer, closely anticipates the early episodes of the Flash Gordon comic strip.

Most intriguing is the product of merging the protagonist of *Gladiator*, Hugo Danner, with the plotline of *When Worlds Collide*. The result is nothing less than Superman (with a capital "S"). Superman's creators, Jerry Siegel and Joe Schuster, are reported to have acknowledged their debt to Wylie and Balmer's works.

As late as 1951, in one of his most accomplished and enduring works, *The Disappearance*, Wylie takes the gender issue as his sole focus. Through a cosmic quirk of unexplained cause, all the females in the world disappear and the males of the species are left to fend for themselves. Simultaneously, in a parallel reality, all the males disappear and the females are left on their own.

It should be noted that Wylie worked in a variety of genres. His novel *The Murderer Invisible* (1931) straddles the fields of crime fiction and science fiction, anticipating the later achievements of Alfred Bester and Isaac Asimov among others. His collaborative (and anonymous) novel *The Smiling Corpse* (1935) is not only a murder mystery but a raucous and devastating satire based on his brief, unhappy stay at the *New Yorker*. Perhaps the scarcest of Wylie's books, although admittedly not important as literature, is *Blondy's Boy Friend* (1930), a little romance written under the pseudonym Leatrice Homesley.

As for *The Savage Gentleman* (1932), it should be only a minor and, one hopes, forgivable "spoiler" to say that this novel centers on the infant Henry Stone, whose father, betrayed by the child's mother, spirits him away to a tropical island. Assisted by two male companions, the senior Stone raises his son to fear, hate, and, above all, never to trust any woman. When Henry, now a young man, returns Tarzan-like to civilization, the plot takes a number of fascinating turns.

The male-bonding aspects of *Savage Gentleman* are of course anticipated in many earlier works, from the stories of David and Jonathan and Jason and the Argonauts to *The Three*

Musketeers, but Wylie's version, especially involving the boy raised without female influence or even presence, seemingly struck a chord in the pulp audience. This audience, largely composed of adolescent males just coming to grips with their own sexuality (and in many cases feeling insecure around females), might have been more comfortable in such a setting than in one that included women.

Pulp historians point out that the themes of *The Savage Gentleman* are replicated to an uncanny degree in the pulp character Clark "Doc" Savage (1933) created by Lester Dent, and then again in the science-fiction series featuring one Curtis Newton aka "Captain Future" (1940) created by Edmond Hamilton. The latter version is noteworthy in that Curtis Newton's three mentors are all inhuman — a metal robot, a rubbery android, and a disembodied brain-in-a-box — yet all three are identified as male.

The Savage Gentleman can be read as a pure adventure story, but in fact it has more to offer the discerning reader whose interests include the psychology and sociology of sex and of race. In the latter regard, Wylie's portrayal of the Negro Jack may be offensive to the modern reader, but it ultimately shows a far greater degree of respect and sympathy than is apparent on the surface.

In his later years Wylie continued to produce fiction and nonfiction, much of the former of a fantastic nature. Like such highly regarded literary figures as Kurt Vonnegut (1922–2007) and Ursula K. Le Guin (b. 1929), Wylie managed to avoid the label "science-fiction writer," and the attendant literary ghettoization, while actually producing great amounts of science fiction. Philip Wylie died October 25, 1971. His last published work, the posthumous *The End of the Dream* (1972), is a grim novel of the future.

chapter
ONE

Within the triangle that is formed by Ceylon, Tasmania, and Madagascar, on a pitch-black night, shortly before the turn of the last century, a steam yacht beat its way against massive seas.

It was a storm-worn vessel. The sails reefed close to its spars were dark and patched. Its brasswork was not bright. Hot sun had blistered its paint, and salt water had stripped it away. Yet these ravages could not conceal the ship's jaunty lines or eradicate the impression of an original luxury — a luxury now being ignored for stern use.

It carried no lights, except the dim radiation on the hurricane bridge. The sharp bow lifted and plunged. The single screw beat the black water to foam, turned in the air, and bit again in fresh swirls of phosphorus-flecked froth.

The light on the bridge sharply illuminated a compass and was reflected upon the countenance of a man at the wheel.

He was a tall, hawklike man. His face was seamed and tan, and the dim illumination glinted on eyes that were like jewels in dark pockets. He wore a heavy ulster and his chin jutted over its collar. He swung with the working of the ship but his stiffly planted feet did not budge. His hands were tight on the wheel. They were white and long-fingered; the man had a seeming of former luxury like that of the yacht.

Eight bells rang on a small ship's clock.

The man leaned forward and peered through the deck housing.

He saw nothing.

Then, abruptly, he began to see. He was looking at the mauled deck before he realized the fact. His horizon expanded with rapidity. The tumultuous scene became visible around him— long ranges of ominous mountains, white-capped and ponderously advancing, and a low-hanging sky that scudded darkly across the other half of his world.

The man's face was statuesque in the fantastic dawn. His lips were taut. His hair was a dark and rugged forest. In his rigidity, he was the image of relentless and unshakable purpose.

He seemed not a man in thought, but one whose thoughts had become stonily transfixed, a man with a grim deed to do, a soldier shot through the heart and still moving forward.

Below decks, in a dim stateroom, a baby cried to the unanswering storm and struggled aimlessly with the rungs that kept it from being thrown to the floor.

A man in an oily cap dozed on a braced kitchen chair that had been placed beside a pounding engine.

A giant Negro opened his eyes and rose, fully dressed. He tottered to the galley and began the difficult operation of preparing coffee.

There was no one else aboard the hell-bound vessel. Green water washed itself from the name on its stern.

It was the *Falcon*. Its port was New York.

The man at the wheel moved his lips. He scrutinized the compass. His gaze was no longer introverted; with every rise of the bridge it scanned the horizon.

The Negro appeared, coffee in a metal bottle; he pulled the door shut against the wind.

"Morning, Mr. Stone."

The man nodded.

"Coffee."

The pilot took the bottle, held it for the Negro to uncork, and drank slowly.

"Mighty bad weather, sir."

"Yes, Jack."

That was all. The door opened again. Wind fanned through the enclosed bridge. The Negro fought his way back toward the galley. He went from there by a companionway to look at the baby. He stood over it for a while, shaking his head.

At eleven o'clock the wind died. A patch of blue appeared in the clouds and their color changed from purple-black to gray and white. At noon the sun shone.

Stone rang to the engine room and the man who had been there joined him.

"Take the wheel, Mr. McCobb."

The Scotchman complied. He bit his down-turned pipe and glanced occasionally at his employer. Stone shot the sun and scrawled on a board.

"Four points east," he said.

At two he came up from a visit to the infant and took the wheel.

"You can go, Mr. McCobb."

An expanding of the lips that was not a smile came on Stone's face when he saw the island. It was, at first, little different from the waves on the remote water — the summit of a blue and vegetated hill. A lost, mist-hung oasis in the desert of the ocean.

The baby slept.

The Negro made sandwiches.

The Scot sat dully beside his engine.

From the sea the island emerged. It presented a narrow promontory, but the rise of hills inland indicated that it was of considerable extent. Immense evergreens grew upon it, interspersed with palms. Its coastline, which the *Falcon* presently skirted, was rocky and precipitous. The water around it was blue, brilliantly blue beneath a sun now hot and white.

Stone steered in shirt sleeves. His eyes followed the coast. He signaled for half speed.

In the engine room the Scotchman jumped at the jangle of the bells. Half speed meant — what? A caprice of the ship's master? Danger?

He did not think of land. In that latitude, no one thought of land.

Stone swung toward an indentation. When he seemed on the verge of colliding with the rocky shore, he swung again.

The outbent greenery almost touched the decks of the yacht. In a moment a broad and long harbor opened before the entering vessel. It was a wild, natural, unpopulated expanse of water. A green bird came as an escort from the forest and sat upon the bulwarks.

The bell jangled for full speed. The *Falcon* gathered momentum and its course was toward a golden beach.

There was no expression in Stone's irrevocable eyes.

When he was five boat lengths from shore he summoned the engineer to the speaking tube.

"On deck, McCobb. We're going aground. You've only a few seconds."

The interval of plate-glass water between ship and shore diminished.

When the *Falcon* hit, part of her bottom went out. Deep furrows of sand turned up on both sides of the bow. Stone was pressed against the wheel. The splintering crash shook boughs in the jungle and echoed from crystalline escarpments on the hills. The baby was thrust against the head of its padded crib and it woke, crying. Steam began to issue from broken pipes with a velvety roar and water rushed into the boiler room.

McCobb had gained the deck in time to discover the yacht in full motion across an unexpected harbor. He saw the oncoming shore and braced himself.

After the shock, he lit his pipe and stared methodically at all parts of the unsalvageable wreck that had been the *Falcon*. Then he walked to the bridge.

Stone was gazing at the island, with his arms spread in exultation. The mold of his long mood had been scorched away. He was like a Crusader who stood at last before the walls of Jerusalem. McCobb regarded him attentively, breathlessly. He knew that the beaching of the *Falcon* represented the attainment of a goal for the ship's master.

But what goal?

Stone's lips moved. "We're here!"

The Scot found himself repeating dully, "Here?" Then he

gripped himself. Everything was trancelike. The spell had been
broken and yet its effect lingered. He cleared his throat and
tapped his pipe on the ledge of a window.

"We're here, Mr. Stone, wherever here is. And we're here to
stay. Stranded. I'm not a curious man by nature— but I think
that since I'm mixed up in this— I should have an explanation.
I trust you'll pardon plain speaking?"

McCobb calculated that his words would jolt Stone into
his senses— unless they had been lost irretrievably. But the
Falcon's owner merely took his arm and led him to the open
bridge.

The sun poured on them and the island lay like jade on all
sides of the wreck.

"It's beautiful," Stone whispered. "Beautiful, beautiful."

McCobb squinted his steel eyes. "It's pretty. And I can believe it's dangerous. These islands sometimes are."

Stone turned. His transfiguration departed somewhat.
"Sorry, McCobb. My soul is overwrought. I'll explain— as much
as I can explain."

At that moment they heard Jack's voice and, turning toward the stern, they saw him. He was clinging to the rail, his
great arms knotty with muscular effort. "I see you," he wailed.
"You're not there, but I see you. I done crossed over Jordan. I
done looked at the promised land."

"Jack!" Stone called.

The Negro presented a melancholy face. "I hear you, too,
boss. We'se dead."

"Nonsense. We've run aground on an island. Talk to him,
McCobb. I'm going to have a look at the baby."

The engineer went down to the deck. He stood beside Jack,
and Jack seemed as tall again as he. "It's all right, Jack. We just
hit shore here."

The Negro shook his head. "I don' know. I don' know. Mr.
Stone must of been mighty restful to run into so much of something after going so long on so little of nothing." The ellipsis of
the observation pleased Jack; he laughed involuntarily.

A smile came and went on McCobb's face. "At any rate, we're safe."

"Yes, boss."

"You better get lunch ready — or breakfast."

"Yes, boss."

McCobb went below. Water had filled the coal bunkers, water had flooded the boiler room — water that would rise and fall with the tides, bringing corrosion and sand and sea urchins. The *Falcon* would never again move.

The forward hatches were dry — or fairly so. The pens that contained the five goats that furnished milk for the baby, and the chickens that occasionally laid eggs for the crew of three, were intact. The goats blaa-ed and the chickens cackled. McCobb wondered if they could smell the land.

He did not understand the deliberate smashing of the ship, but he had a feeling that he should understand it, that the clues to comprehension were in his possession. It was certainly more than a gesture, assuredly a plan. It explained why Stone had sailed from Aden with but two men aboard.

McCobb finished his survey. The sound of steam was dying. The danger of fire had passed. He returned to the bridge and opened a large book of charts. His eye transferred the position Stone had marked on a small map to the general map of the Indian Ocean.

He located the island, roughly. Then he looked for trade routes. There was a route from Albany to Aden. One from Ceylon to Cape Town. One from Cape Town to Batavia. None came within two days' steaming of this remote speck of land. He had expected that. McCobb had followed marine engines through the seven seas for twenty years, and he would have heard of this isle if any man had heard of it, if any ship had been in the place, if there were a reason to take a ship there or a hope that a ship might go that way.

There was a body of water as large as North America and a few vessels skirted its edges, but none penetrated the center. None.

Nothing.

He closed the book.

Stone came up to the bridge. He sat down. He was smoking a cigar. He could scarcely keep his eyes from the emerald wall outdoors.

"I see you've investigated our— isolation."

"I have."

"You find it— "

"Excessive," McCobb answered and smiled ironically.

Stone laughed. "You're right. Quite right." He dropped ashes from his cigar. "A few years ago I took a party around the world. We cut across here— just for fun— just because we were all good sailors. One night I was at the wheel and there was no other watch. The moon was full. Everyone slept. I kept the *Falcon* on her course and suddenly I was shocked— terrified— to catch a shape out of the corner of my eye.

"It was this island. We passed it at a distance of less than a mile. I caught a glimpse of this wide bay through the opening. I saw the rocky hill yonder. And I was on the verge of waking everyone when something made me stop. I realized that no other man on earth had seen this place. I shared a knowledge of it with— the gods. So, instead of calling everyone, I put down the position accurately and I sailed on. I'd lost sight of it, dreaming, before I realized that my approach had been dangerous. There might have been reefs."

McCobb held a match to his pipe.

Stone continued in an enthralled voice. "The thing never left me. Year after year I thought of going back. I imagined myself wrecked there. I even amused myself by making lists of what I would require for a long stay there. Then— "

"Then?"

Stone moved to the steps that led to the deck and looked away from McCobb. "You're a silent devil. How much do you know about me? I mean— aside from the fact that I own the *New York Morning Record*? That I own a string of banks? That I have a fine yacht? Know the right people? . . . How much?"

"Very little, sir."

"Stone. We'll drop the 'sir' — you and I." He was quiet for a moment. Then he turned. "Did you know I was married?"

"I did."

"Did you know my wife's name?"

"Nellie Larsen."

"Yes."

McCobb walked to the windows and stared at the island. He knew that he would find the answer to the mystery of their arrival in the next few moments. He saw that Stone was distressed. He prompted in a slow voice:

"I was sitting at a cafe in Paris, once, when she passed. Everyone stood and gaped. 'There goes Nellie Larsen,' they said. Her horses stopped to let an old woman cross. She sat there, pale as an angel. Blossoms from the horse-chestnut trees fell on her and stuck in her hair. Then she drove on. I remembered her."

Stone's hands were clenched and white. "You remembered her. And so shall I. We were so happy, McCobb, that it could not last. Yes — it could. She went away."

McCobb murmured. He did not say words, but Stone was given to understand by the sound that McCobb knew about her going away.

"When I reached my house that day," he said hoarsely, "she was not there. I called up the stairs and I laughed. I thought she was out. Then — her maid — just — hinted. I went everywhere. I ran my horses to foam. I had a revolver. But she'd gone far and fast — with a man whose name shall never pass my lips.

"I was wild. The thought is still intolerable. I sat for a long stretch of alternating dark and light beside our son — ours no longer but only mine. I did not know what to do. I could not face my friends. If anyone had said, 'Too bad,' in those days, I would have killed that person.

"Suddenly I remembered this island. I knew, then. And I knew another thing — I knew that my son was going to be brought up to young manhood without the influence of women. Without the knowledge of women, which they imbue in men. I knew. So I began to get ready."

Tears had scalded Stone's cheeks. The Scot was watching the green birds that had now come to the ship in numbers.

Stone checked his emotion. "When you signed that contract — you must have expected — something."

McCobb shrugged. "I did it with my eyes open."

"The last step — was beaching the *Falcon* here. We'll be here — a long time."

"A long time."

"You don't think anyone will find us, do you?"

McCobb smoked. "Someone might come tomorrow. No one will come, in all probability, for years. Years. Years."

"So I thought. It's going to be a glorious adventure, McCobb!"

"And arduous. And tedious."

"At any rate — there's no turning back." Stone stood up. "Now — for the island. We'll explore the shore here. It seems to rise a bit almost at once. Perhaps we can build very near."

"Build?"

"Build!" Stone took his engineer's arm. "A fine house with a stockade around it and a big cellar to store the things I have brought. A pen for the goats and one for the chickens. A garden, by and by. A sawmill and a little blacksmith shop. We won't want for the materials. I have everything. This is no inadvertent and makeshift shipwreck. This is a planned arrival, a deliberate colonization. Come!"

Some of Stone's spirit infected McCobb. His square face lighted. "It may not be so bad," he said slowly.

Jack banged the dinner gong at that instant. The two men went side by side toward the salon.

"What about him?" McCobb asked, as they walked.

Stone gestured with his hands. "Jack? I found Jack in a blind pig in Hampton Roads. He was drunk. He had a chair by the leg. There were two coppers on the floor and three still trying for him. He was laughing and yelling. I never saw such a splendid specimen. He must be pure stock. I said, 'Put that chair down, son.'" Stone chuckled and led McCobb into the salon ahead of himself. "He put it down. 'Come on,' I said. He grinned and sobered a bit. 'Yes, boss,' he answered. It cost me two hundred dollars to square things. I saved him a nice stretch in the pen. But— now— Jack's my slave."

McCobb nodded. The floor of the salon was canted, but not so much that they could not sit down at the table. Jack came with a tray of food. He served them and then stood still. It was not like him. Both men were aware of his curiosity.

Stone looked at him. "Something on your mind, Jack?"

"No, boss."

"What is it?"

"How long are we going to be here, boss?"

"I don't know. A long time."

"Yes, boss."

"Years, maybe."

Jack chuckled. "That's a real long time. Yes, indeed. That's a right long time."

He departed, holding his tray over his head. When he returned with meat and potatoes he appeared to have reflected further. "I was thinking this was a bad accident, boss. Mighty bad. Can't clean out the water. Can't push her off. I was thinking— "

It was obvious that the dim resources of Jack's subconscious were grappling with the possibility that the accident might have been deliberate. But he was incapable of realizing the fact of their position. A mere suspicion kept him agitated.

Stone allayed it. "Don't worry about the boat. It's no good now. We're going to build a house on shore and move there. I want you to watch the baby this afternoon. Don't leave the room at all. I'll give you a gun. We won't be far away. But we're going ashore to see what's what."

"Yes, boss."

Stone jumped down on the sand. McCobb followed. They crossed the beach. At the edge of the forest-jungle they looked back. The *Falcon* lay in the sand, her decks sloped and her funnel awry. They heard Jack's voice singing to the baby. McCobb shivered from a combination of sentiments he could not describe.

They rounded a screw palm, walked through a clump of ferns, and vanished. The trunks of ebony trees and tall evergreens rose around them. Through the trees ran nets of flowering vines. Moss hung from them and their lofty foliage blotted out the sun and held in a deep quiet. The silence, however, was more illusion than fact, for it was constantly pervaded by the hum of insects and the chirp and flutter of birds. A broad and brilliant butterfly settled on a waxy orchid.

Then, in their path, a mottled coil moved slowly and the head of a snake was raised. Stone fired at it. The coils threshed.

"That's a big one," McCobb said softly.

They watched it die. "Not as big as it might be," Stone answered. "It's a boa."

The ground rose to a miniature plateau over which the forest green was spread on mighty boles. On the western slope of the plateau they heard the sound of water and came upon a lusty brook that ran down toward the sea. Its water was clear and in a still pool they saw a swarm of multicolored fish.

Behind the plateau was thick brush. On the eastern side it fell away again to a tangle broken by huge boulders.

They went back to the top of the plateau. It was perhaps twenty acres in extent.

Stone regarded it. "This is in the right place as far as winds are concerned. And it's not far from the *Falcon* — "

McCobb nodded. "So I was thinking. The small stuff by the brook will make a good stockade. We can cut a road to the beach and put corduroy on the sand. Then — maybe we could get the winch up here and rig a boiler."

"The winch?"

"Sure. We could use it to pull a sort of stone boat over our road. A railway to the ship. See what I mean?"

"By George!" Stone exclaimed.

"Afterward we could haul rocks from the brook with it. Rocks for a cellar and chimneys. If we can dig here — "

"If we can't dig, we can blast."

"So we can. It will take time."

"But it will be worth it." Stone stared up at the trees. In the distance a small band of what were presumably monkeys scurried and gibbered through the leaves. "If we took down about fifty trees — we'd have quite a clearing."

"And a view," the Scot added. In the presence of this prospect of creative work, his mind had become entirely objective. He paced through the shadows. "The cellar here. The chimneys there and there. You have cement? Good. And if you can saw — why — there's no limit to what we can do. We can build a private Taj Mahal. I imagine Jack is kind of an engine in himself. It'll give us something to think about — in any event."

Stone nodded his head in affirmation. His expression, as he regarded McCobb, was one almost of relief. The engineer had admirably withstood the shock of his arrival on the island. Stone had considered other possibilities — the man might have been savagely angry, might even have turned murderous. He might have failed absolutely to comprehend the motives that led to the shipwreck. He might have been swept by despair and proved helpless and useless.

Stone had not expected those things — he understood the men who went to sea and he understood also the temperament of the Scotch — but he was none the less freed of a burden.

They made their way back to the ship, moving warily and with distrust. They thought of the boa with every step. They thought of other things to which they later gave voice.

When they came on board, Jack sprang from below decks. He had discarded his gun and in his hand was a sinister knife.

Stone smiled. "Hello, Jack."

"Yes, boss?"

"See anything?"

"No, sir."

"Hear anything?"

"I hear lots of things in the woods. But I don't see anything."

"Good. You can get dinner, now. We're going to start to work this afternoon over on the island. We'll work two at a time. You and I, or McCobb and I, or you and McCobb."

"Yes, boss."

"Baby asleep?"

"Yes, indeed. That's the sleepinest baby I ever saw. First he sleeps on one side. Then he wakes up and if you put him on the other he goes to sleep again. He can't seem to do nothing but sleep."

"Good. It's going to be hard work."

Jack showed his teeth. He hesitated and then asked an oblique question: "I heard a shot— or maybe I didn't hear no shot."

"That was a shot."

"Trying out the guns?"

"Snake," Stone said.

Jack stiffened a little but his smile did not fade. "That's what I thought."

The setting sun had brought a little wind from the sea. Mc-Cobb stood on the broken stern and sniffed it. He took out his tobacco and filled his pipe reluctantly. All afternoon he had been plagued by the thought that soon he would cease smoking. He sighed.

His mind ran in a medley that was partly irregular because of fatigue and partly stirred by the variety of experiences he had undergone during the day. He thought about Stone's opinion of women. It must have been due to the fact that Stone had had very little experience with women. There was, McCobb's daydream reminded him, a Malay girl who had worn a flower in her hair, and an Irish trollop in San Pedro, and a girl with devious eyes who had called to him on the street in Buenos Aires. These women were all bad, but their badness had not affected him the way the flight of one woman had affected Stone.

He was too hard. Too idealistic. Too impetuous. Too much a man of brain and too little a man of honest passions. There was a girl here and a girl there, McCobb's senses whispered.

Now there would be no more girls.

No more.

He might die here. He discarded that thought. He had a certain faith in Stone's brain. That faith had increased during the afternoon when he had assisted in the unloading of the first, forward hatch. It had contained precisely what they would need to commence their siege for occupation of the island. Precisely. Nothing missing. Stone was a great organizer.

McCobb whispered pipe-smoke into the air and watched it make a personal cloud against the soft indigo of the harbor and the uplifted verdure of the island.

The hills were rank with growth. They had a luster. They were ominous and pregnant. They had been sitting there for thousands and thousands of years generating their own life. Now they were invaded. Now man had come there.

How big was the island? Three or four miles in diameter, perhaps. What lived on it? Insects, birds, monkeys, snakes. What else? Who knew? There came a coughing from the forest, and a dismal wail; McCobb's spine tingled. It grew dark.

Stone was in his quarters. He unlocked an immense book, dipped a pen, and began to write. His brow was lined and his fingers slowly traced long sentences.

"November 3rd, 1898. After leaving Aden, where I made the preparations already detailed here, I proceeded south and east to the island mentioned in a foregoing portion of the diary and, after a stormy passage, sighted it early this morning. The harbor I had previously glimpsed was deep and ended in a fairly precipitous beach upon which I ran the *Falcon* under a full head of steam."

He adjusted the oil lamp and continued. "My plan thus culminated, I hastened to explore the immediate shore line, after finding the spirits of my engineer to be good and the Negro's reaction puzzled but in no way overwhelmed. It — the shore — rose in a small hill that lent itself admirably for a building site, inasmuch as it is protected from the south and east by a small mountain and is surrounded by large trees.

"We have commenced unloading. The baby appears to be in fine health and sleeps most of the time under heavy mosquito bars. He has become quite accustomed to goat's milk and is both ruddy and fat. Sometimes I feel that I have done him an injustice, but when I fasten my mind upon . . ." Stone halted a full minute before he filled the blank: ". . . Nellie, I know that I am doing all — the only thing — that could be done under the circumstances. *The child must never be told our shipwreck here was intentional.* With expectations of future tranquility, with a zestful interest in the possibilities of our new home, with faith and hope, we commit ourselves to Providence."

Stone locked away the sententious words. Like almost every man of action, he was self-conscious and awkward when he wrote, and he had never furnished any other copy to his newspaper than an occasional heavy editorial. It was policy and growth that had interested him. But now, he felt that it was essential to keep a certain record.

He went to sleep after a brief walk on deck — a walk that was punctuated by listenings, occasional frowns of perplexity, and nods. He slept more steadily and more deeply than he had slept for many months.

A shout woke him.

His feet hit the floor. The baby whimpered in the basket that hung above his bunk.

The shout came again. It was Jack.

Stone was on deck in an instant, the door shut behind him, a revolver in his hand.

"Go on!" Jack yelled into the darkness. "Get out of here. We don' want you. Beat it!"

"What's up, Jack?"

"Ho— Jack!" McCobb's voice cut through the darkness.

They met amidships.

"It was a man," Jack said. Stone's heart stopped.

"Go on."

"That's all. A man. A big man with blue eyes. Hairy. I was lying in my bed looking at the stars and he came to the door. I grabs a butcher knife that happens to be under my pillow. 'Go 'way!' I says."

"I heard you," Stone muttered absently.

"He went. Plumb off the ship and as quiet as a cat."

"Are you sure it was a man?"

"Yes, boss. Leastwise it might of been a woman."

"Which way did it go?"

"In them woods where you're fixing to have a house."

McCobb and Stone stared into the murk.

"There was something mighty funny about that man," Jack said, almost to himself and in a trembling voice. "Something mighty funny. I seen it at the time, but now I can't recollect what it was."

Stone turned. His tone was hard. "Try to remember."

"I forget."

"Did it carry a spear?"

"No, boss."

"Did it walk on its hands and feet?"

"No, boss. It was a-standin' at the door."

"Did it have a top-knot? Or lips that stuck out? Or a hat on? Or clothes? Or a feather in its hair?"

Jack shook his head. Surprise had routed his memory. "I can't say what it had, but what it had was mighty funny."

"Something people don't usually have?"

Jack's eyes rolled whitely in the starlight. "Something I ain't never seen on no pusson before. But I can't recall. It come quick-like an' it went quicker when it seen that there knife that was lying accidentally under my pillow."

"Never mind the knife. Go back, Jack, and try to sleep. Keep your door shut. If it comes again, shoot. Don't fool around with a knife."

"I ain't much on guns, I— "

"You shoot."

"Yes, boss."

Stone and McCobb went toward the bow of the stranded *Falcon*. Stone's silhouette towered over the shadow of his engineer, even as Jack towered above Stone.

"I hadn't given much thought to savages," Stone admitted.

McCobb's voice reflected his temper. "I hadn't given any."

"Of course, it's possible."

"And then— Jack may have been mistaken."

There was a pause. Stone ended it. "Anyhow— he saw something."

"No doubt of that."

"Perhaps we better have a watch. You become so accustomed to security on a ship that you forget your vulnerability when you're aground."

"I'll watch first."

"Right."

McCobb lit his pipe. His hands were as steady as rock. Stone hesitated before he re-entered his cabin. "By the way— I noticed you smoked and I brought along a big supply of tobacco in airtight tins. Besides that— there's some seed— so you don't need to stint yourself."

"Thanks," McCobb said, in quick and suppressed tone. The door closed. "Thanks," the Scot repeated, and sat down with his rifle across his knees. It passed through his mind that there were worse things than being lost at the bottom of the globe with Stephen Stone.

The forest on the plateau had been opened so that a vast square of it was illuminated by the sun. Around the edges of the square was a stockade with two gates. One gate led toward the brook and one made a passage for the road that ran to the beach a hundred yards away. The top of the stockade was strung with five strands of barbed wire.

Smoke unfolded itself softly from the chimney of the boiler that fed steam to the winch, which puffed and rattled under the manipulations of Stephen Stone. A taut cable was reeled in slowly and it brought over the rough road a sort of sled on which was piled gear from the hatches of the *Falcon*.

When the sled had entered the stockade, Stone shut the gate and began to unload it.

He was naked to the waist. His trousers were stuffed in leather boots. His shoulders were tanned by the sun. When he lifted, muscles rose and undulated on his body. A more powerful spectacle was presented by Jack, however. Under his brown skin, as he raised stones up on the chimney scaffold, a torrent of oiled strength bulged and slid. He grinned and sometimes sang as he worked.

The baby sat in its basket in the shade of a small bush. Around the basket was a screen. A similar protection had been made for the chickens, and the goats sunned themselves beneath a steel unloading net.

There was a rifle within reach of each man. They had revolvers in their belts. A box of ammunition lay open on the cement foundations of the house. It was obvious that they did not trust their new environment — although they had been working in it for four weeks and no untoward incident had occurred.

"I'll take that big flat one," McCobb called from his perch on the chimney.

"This one?" Jack asked.

"The one next to it."

Jack lifted the stone. McCobb scraped up a trowel full of cement and slapped it against the rock. He fidgeted it in place, put on more cement, and turned toward Stone.

"I can get along without Jack, now, for a while."

"Right. We'll drag the sled back and get another load."

The corral gate opened and closed. McCobb slapped at a purple fly that had landed on his neck. He, alone, wore a shirt. He began to whistle and when the baby made a sound he talked to it.

The steam winch had been invaluable. It acted as elevator, railroad, wagon, plow, stone carrier, and log mover. It pulled whatever was needed into the stockade.

Next, McCobb thought, looking at the walled cellar, which rose to sturdy foundations and the two tall chimneys, they would start the saw and cut wood. Two-by-fours for studding. Inch-thick boards for walls inside and out. Soon after that they would have a house. A big house, with five rooms and a porch. With a view of the bay. A house that had been painted — he had seen the paint come up on the sled, two barrels of it.

It would be a rather fine place to live.

On the *Falcon* Stone dropped into the hold, rolled a keg to the sling, and gave word to Jack, who hoisted it on a block and tackle, swung it outboard, and dropped it to the sled.

Jack sang. Stone found himself whistling.

When the load was complete, they walked back to the stockade. McCobb came down from the chimney scaffold to let them in. The winch rattled again. Jack lifted stones. The scene was not much different from any construction — save for the richness of the foliage in the background, the firearms, and the rough logs and poles that made the scaffold on which McCobb worked.

Late in the afternoon Stone went out alone. A small boat was moored beside the *Falcon*. There was a larger craft, equipped with sails, still on the davits, but that was reserved for a later day.

Stone pushed off the small boat and rowed some distance out on the bay. His eyes constantly searched the shore line as he moved through the water. He saw nothing.

After he had satisfied himself that he was far enough off shore he took a jointed rod from beneath his seat, set it up, strung it with a line, affixed a reel, and baited with an artificial lure. He propped the pole in the stern, let out line, and began to troll slowly.

He had rowed perhaps a dozen strokes when the pole bent, the line cut water, and the reel screamed.

He grabbed his tackle. Stone had caught salmon in New Brunswick and tarpon in the Gulf. What he had now was in no way inferior to those fish.

It made a long, determined rush. He slowed it with his thumb and the boat began to move in answer to the pull. The fish gave up after a fairly long run and broke water three times. It was large and slender, silver-backed with rose splotches. He could see it plainly the third time and while he was still wondering about its identity it went under the boat.

He whipped his pole around the stern. His only thought was to save his tackle. He realized that he should have brought stronger weapons to the conquest of the unfished bay. For five minutes he resisted an attempt of the fish to get into the open sea. Then came the surrender. It was compromised when he reached down to pull it from the water by a last rush, but in another minute he had it aboard.

He rowed back, still watching the shore. He tied the skiff. He walked with the fish and his rifle to the stockade. He had been gone just twenty minutes.

McCobb shouted from the chimney. "Luck already?"

Stone felt a stirring of pride that supplemented the elation he had known while the conflict was in progress.

"Something for supper." He slammed the gate.

McCobb whistled. "Something indeed."

Jack took the fish. He grinned. "That'll taste mighty good."

The Scotchman counted out loud. "Let's see. There were the ducks. And those grouse— or whatever they were. And the oysters. The clams and the turtle. That fish makes the sixth natural contribution to our larder— in the way of meat. If you include the fruit— "

Stone nodded. "Not so bad, eh? And when we get a garden going. Peas and beans and carrots and beets and potatoes and almost anything else you can name." He turned to Jack. "You go down and fix the fish. I think if you stuff a midsection with bread and onions and roast it— "

"Yes, boss. Got to milk first."

They watched him enter the goat pen. Jack's relations with the three dams and the two rams were the relations of a man to his equals. He had names for all five. Miss Susie. Linda. Clara. Little Joe and Snake Eyes. Snake Eyes had once butted him rather forcefully, and the talk he gave to the goat, the anxiety and grief he expressed, had kept Stone and McCobb in silent mirth for a whole evening.

Milk rang on the side of his shining pail.

McCobb and Stone continued with their work. When Jack had gone they chuckled.

"Must be wonderful to be black," McCobb said.

Stone arranged tarpaulins on his stores. "Must be."

"Never disconcerted. Never so frightened you can't laugh a minute later. Faithful. It's amazing."

They looked at each other. It passed through their minds simultaneously that they were forming an intense friendship. There was no need to talk about it— no need to talk about anything except the casual points of conversation, which made hard work, day after day, into a sort of pleasure.

In another four weeks the sawmill was voicing its nasal menace to the forest. Planks emerged from the spinning disk like cake slices. Log after log of hardwood gave itself up. The two-by-fours were already in place, forming the skeleton of the house, with holes where the doors and windows were to be and a geometrical slant of roof. Window glass and ready-made frames had been brought from the *Falcon*.

The baby sat in his basket in the shade. The goats were about their continual experiments with the local vegetation and grass. The chickens laid regularly.

In January, McCobb began to lay flooring. In February, he finished the outside sheathing. In March, they had lined the inside with vertical boards. The boards on the exterior ran horizontally and overlapped, like clapboards. The work once again became diversified.

Jack thatched with palm leaves over the wooden roof. Stone fitted the bunks from the *Falcon* into the three bedrooms. McCobb painted.

Before long, the entire contents of the yacht would have been transferred to the house. In the cellar were forty large copper drums that had been filled with materials they would need in years ahead and from which the air had been exhausted. In the cellar also was a vast supply of wines and spirits. A smaller building of stone housed the tools in use. The library of the *Falcon* had been transferred to the large general room. It was an enormous library, noteworthy for the completeness of its reference works and educational volumes as well as for its absolute lack of fiction in any form. Also they had moved a vast stock of drugs and medicines.

There was a multitude of unpacked boxes and crates and barrels, the contents of which would be revealed at some less busy time.

The *Falcon* was beginning to show more than her emptiness. All the glass had been taken from her bridge. The ports would follow when they moved. Brass railing was gone and the hardware from many of the doors and windows. In due time, stripped to the bone, she would become nothing more than a reservoir of metal — a mine, a source of supply. The gear would go first, then the canted funnel, then parts of the engine.

For a time the dismantlement of the ship had depressed

McCobb, even though he knew that it would be impossible to float her, hopeless to try to repair her. But gradually his interest was transferred from the ship to the house. He knew that when the house was in order, interest would be then turned to the mysterious island behind the stockade, which remained silent, almost unresisting, and wholly unknown.

They moved officially in April.

They had their first taste of wine that night. McCobb and Stone sat at the table. Jack beamed and served.

Stone lifted his glass. "Thanks, McCobb. Here's health."

McCobb bowed. "Here's luck, sir."

The baby cooed in the stronghold they had made for him.

After the meal they went out on the veranda and sat in comfortable chairs behind screens that shut out the humming insects.

Their reflections were varied and they gave partial and random voice to them.

"We might almost be within an hour of civilization," McCobb said.

Silence.

"I wonder what's going on in Little Old New York tonight?" Stone had never uttered that thought before, although he had doubtless entertained it.

"It isn't night in New York."

Both men chuckled.

Silence.

"Ever have anything to do with natives, McCobb?"

"Savages?"

"Yes."

McCobb drew on his pipe and it bubbled. "I have. The bushmen in Australia. The Senegalese in Africa."

"Doesn't it seem strange to you that they would send one deputy to search us and then never appear again?"

"Not like anything I ever heard of. They're either hostile or else curious. I don't think aborigines of any kind would hide for months like this."

"Odd."

Silence again.

Jack began to play his banjo in the kitchen. He added his voice to the music. The appearance of the banjo was a nine-day wonder on the island — and a very acceptable wonder.

Stone lifted his voice. "Come on out here on the porch, Jack."

He came, reluctantly, and they were compelled to beg him to play. Finally they desisted and he sat as long as he felt politeness demanded. It was only after he had returned to the kitchen that flavor was restored to the music.

"Funny beggar," Stone murmured.

"I've known worse," McCobb said. It was not necessary for Stone to agree out loud.

The rains had started late in April— rains of the southeast monsoon— but they had been light and infrequent, although the sky was generally cloudy for days at a time. The house had been put in shape for them, however, and the three men went ahead with work on its interior whenever the weather hampered outdoor activities.

By midsummer for the northern hemisphere, and what amounted to midwinter for them, they had all the major details complete. It was then, and only then, that in the two white men, at least, a vague spirit of restlessness appeared.

McCobb noticed it in Stone when he found him staring at the rocky summit of the small mountain that rose behind the house. But McCobb did not notice it in himself when he became petulant over the fact that the iron runners he had carefully made for the winch sled did not fit.

Stone found him glaring at the metal strips, spitting disgustedly and swearing under his breath.

He grinned. "Why don't you kick them, McCobb?"

"Hell! They're too short."

"Well— we'll make a new sled. It's easier."

"Yes."

They looked at each other and laughed. That day at lunch Stone said: "You know, it's getting to be about time for us to do a little exploring around the place. I was looking at the hill the other day. It wouldn't be much of a trick to climb it."

McCobb was surprised at the intensity of his impulse. "That's an excellent idea! I've been itching to get out and around for weeks."

"Feel shut in?"

"Well— "

"Why not admit it? I do. But I didn't want to go out and look for trouble until we were comfortable here. The rest of the island could wait on us."

McCobb ate in silence for a moment. "What was your impression of the size and shape of the island when you saw it from the sea?"

"Just what I gave you when we first discussed it. Vague. It wasn't very large— although I couldn't see it all on account of the relative feebleness of the moonlight. Coming in this time, it was misty. I think it's about four miles long, running north and south, and perhaps three miles and a half wide."

"There ought to be a good many interesting things and places, then."

"We'll see."

They walked out of the stockade side by side. Jack shut the gate behind them. McCobb felt his nerves tingling.

"I'm excited," he said, in a tone that did not appear to contain any emotion whatever.

"So am I."

Stone led the way around the wooden, wire-topped wall. At its rear, he broke into the green riot of vegetation. He went gingerly, in spite of the fact that he was shod in knee-high leather boots. He carried his rifle in the crook of his arm, and its trigger was set on the safety catch.

The ground behind the house descended at first into a sort of valley filled with deep ferns. Insects hummed there and birds flew overhead. They saw a small monkey at a distance, and one of the boas with which they had become familiar moved lazily from their path.

On the opposite side of the vale the trees grew thick and vines ran between them so that they were forced to hack their way in places. A steady rise commenced and with every hundred yards the walking conditions improved. Eventually Stone stopped and pointed.

The trees thinned. A few rods distant from them, they were supplanted by grass as high as the armpits of a tall man. They hastened to the edge of this unexpected prairie. A broad, rolling savannah dotted here and there with clumps of trees opened before them to the base of the mountain.

It was much like the African veldt and, while they were looking, a herd of animals moved up over a small rise.

"Good Lord!" McCobb whispered.

Stone gripped his arm. "Those are a kind of zebu. Little ones. The ancestors of cows."

The men waited in the shadow while the herd approached. The creatures were certainly cowlike, although their legs were slender and on their backs they had a large hump. They were led by a bull and presently they stopped to graze. They ate with a continual switching of their tails and a frequent uplifting of their broad, bland faces.

Stone stepped from cover and whistled. The heads shot up. They stared in stony immobility at the men. But when the men did not make any further sign, they recommenced their browsing.

"That doesn't look as if there were natives," Stone murmured.

"Shall we get one?"

"On the way back."

"Will it be safe to cross the plain? Maybe they'll charge."

Stone considered. Finally he began walking toward the animals. They gave him a casual attention until he was within a hundred yards, then, slowly, they began to walk away from him.

"It's all right," Stone called, and, with the sound of his voice, the zebu-oxen increased their walk to a lumbering trot.

Stone and McCobb went across the grassy plain gaily.

"Meat," Stone almost shouted. "By George! McCobb, there's fine meat there. And I wouldn't be surprised if you could domesticate the damn things. Milk them, maybe."

"And the hides. So far," McCobb said exultantly, "I've seen only monkey fur for our feet. But we can make real leather out of those hides and real shoes. Chaps, too, and boots."

They plunged into the green ring that encircled the base of the mountain. It was difficult to cross, filled with boulders that had dropped down the steep sides, and thick with a long-thorned brier. Snakes lived among the rocks, but already they had learned not to waste ammunition on snakes. A staff five or six feet in length served their purpose.

They sweated and toiled over the uneven ground, making their way constantly upward. The discovery of the animals on the plain had led them to expect many more surprises. And, with the moment near when they would know the precise size and shape of their island, they felt an increasing tension.

McCobb, especially, held in his mind a picture of an islet three miles in diameter, of which every nook and cranny could be explored in a few days and that would furnish nothing afterward to break the monotony of their long confinement. His hopes alternately triumphed over and fell prey to his fears. When they had finally worked their way through the green belt and could look back, he turned his head with an unbearable emotion.

He was depressed. The treetops fell away steeply below them. The plain of the zebus was perhaps a mile long and a quarter of a mile wide. Beyond it, and farther north, was the forest that ran to the shore, a blue blur coiling from the chimney of the house that made a white square in the trees, a glint of bay, a view of the stern of the *Falcon*, looking from the mountainside like a toy, and the sea. To the west, cliffs fell into the sea. A shoulder of the mountain shut out the view eastward and the bulk of the mountain itself lay between them and the south.

"It's gorgeous," Stone said thoughtfully.

"Yes," McCobb replied. "Let's get up to the top."

They scrambled up igneous ledges. They paused to marvel at huge, weather-worn outcroppings of crystals. They skirted a precipice that was fully a hundred feet in height and they came to a rocky shelf where nothing grew and from which, they knew, the top would be reached by a moment's effort.

They stopped. McCobb looked at the pinnacle above.

"Give you a leg up," Stone said.

The Scot shook his head. "No. I'll boost you. I haven't the courage to look for myself."

Stone understood. "It may be a terrible disappointment," he admitted. "I'll go."

McCobb bent down and Stone stood on his back. McCobb felt the pressure of the feet diminish and depart. He shut his eyes. There was a silence so long that McCobb could not endure it.

"What do you see?" he called.

"Come on." Stone's face appeared at the edge of the short declivity and McCobb knew by its expression that it was not disappointment that awaited him. He took the down-reaching hands and was lifted bodily onto a little, flat summit.

He looked from the sitting posture in which he had arrived. He gasped. He swore softly.

The entire island spread beneath their gaze. It was the shape of a sting ray with a forked tail— and the fork was their bay. They had built their house at the end of the "tail"— at the end of a long and narrow peninsula that had given Stone his idea of the island's dimensions.

Actually, the main body of the island ran north and south for at least fifteen miles. From east to west it stretched some twenty miles. The pinnacle on which they sat was its highest point.

A rim of rock ran along the southern shore. The land was half savannah— like the stretch through which they had made their way— and half thick jungle and forest. But in the center of the main body of the island was a large lake. The new green of the grasses, the darker sheens of the trees, the blue of the lake, the tawny colors of the coastal rocks and beaches, and above all, the indigo of the surrounding sea made a magnificent spectacle.

McCobb thrilled with an emotion almost religious. Here was beauty, adventure, variety, area. Above all— area. Space to move in, space to investigate, and an end of the oppressive feeling of smallness.

Then he looked at Stone and Stone was standing on the rock, his mane of dark hair blowing, his gaunt face set, and tears on his cheeks.

They remained there for more than an hour, drinking in the extent of their kingdom. Then they made separate analyses of the territory. They talked a little and mentioned especially that there was no sign of human habitation, no smoke except their own, no clearings or village visible.

After that they went back.

On the prairie they relocated the herd of zebu-oxen and Stone's rifle brought one to earth. They carried away as much meat as they could and presently they returned to the stockade.

That night their spirits knew no bounds. They told Jack a hundred times what they had found, and Jack vaguely realized its significance. They ate the fresh meat with gusto, and uttered unreasonable praise of its qualities.

And that night, after dinner, McCobb gave voice to his one remaining doubt. He spoke to Stone when they were on the wide porch.

"There's one little thing," he began, "that I can mention now. I couldn't speak of it until we had reached an understanding of each other. But everything has turned out so well— "

Stone prompted him. "What is it?"

"I like it here. I like the life. It's making a man of me. I like you. I like Jack. I don't mind staying fifteen or twenty years, if twenty are necessary. When I get back I'll have enough money to keep me the rest of my life. If I hadn't come here I'd have probably married a shrew"— he was alarmed by that inadvertent statement, but Stone only laughed— "and settled into a little hell called home.

"But since we landed here I've known something that you have done but not mentioned."

"Yes?" Stone's voice was placid.

The Scotchman smoked in silence for a time. "Just exactly how long will we stay here?"

"Why — you know as much about that as I do."

An inner fear sounded in McCobb's words. "There isn't any real reason for keeping me in suspense. You know the day. You planned everything so perfectly that certainly you've left in New York or somewhere — even in several places" — McCobb laughed with a heartiness he did not quite feel — "instructions to be opened in fifteen or twenty years. Instructions telling the opener how to rescue us, giving the position of the island and funds to send an expedition here."

When the tall man did not speak, McCobb continued: "I know your type of man. You wouldn't throw yourself and your son away when there was such an easy and sure method of accomplishing this isolation for education and of making a return sure."

No answer.

"What about it, Stone?"

McCobb peered through the dark. "Stone!"

He leaped to his feet. He went to Stone's side. Stone had fainted — and McCobb knew that there was one thing of which the great organizer had not thought. Even while he unbuttoned Stone's shirt and felt his faltering heart, the Scot looked over the sea and thought icily that it would someday ripple beside the grave of an old, old man who had been himself.

"Stone!" he shouted. "Jack!"

New York was loud and hot. Horse cars rattled over the cross-town tracks. A steam engine pounded on the elevated railway and ground to a stop. The sound of hoofs beat on the cobble-stones. Wagon wheels, iron-tired, set up a continuous rumble and among the wagons moved broughams and victorias.

In an office building on Park Row that was not a skyscraper but that was high enough to overlook Brooklyn Bridge, two men were greeting each other.

One was Elihu Whitney, the most famous corporation law-yer in Gotham. The other was a Mr. Harriman.

The lawyer wore a Prince Albert — its black coat falling to his knees. His collar was high and his tie black and narrow, knotted crosswise on his starched bosom.

Mr. Harriman carried a bowler in his hand. His suit was light and very tight. In one of the two buttonholes on his coat lapel was a rose. His vest also had lapels, which were buttoned together two inches below his collar.

Mr. Whitney's voice was basso and meticulous: "A fine day, indeed, my dear Harriman. I'm delighted to see you."

Harriman stroked his giant mustache. "A pleasure. May I tender my congratulations on the return of your son and your charming daughter-in-law? A happy couple. One envies these youngsters their honeymoons, eh?"

Whitney chuckled. "Two birds in a bush could not be hap-pier." He bowed and waved his friend to a chair. He pulled a bell cord and an office boy brought a box of cigars. The men helped themselves. The lawyer struck a match on the sole of his shoe and held it for his guest.

"Your son is brilliant," Harriman continued. "Very brilliant. I wish you would convey Mrs. Harriman's salutations to them and tell them that we are both going to call as soon as they can bear to have their nest disturbed."

"They'll be delighted."

"I read so much about them in the *Record*."

"Yes, yes," Whitney said. He patted the underside of his cheek whiskers with the back of his hand and wondered how soon Harriman would reach the point.

The other man drew on the floor with his cane. "The *Record* has depreciated since— ah— Stone left, don't you think?"

A glint came in Whitney's eye. Harriman had come to talk about Stone. The lawyer would have offered odds at his club that Mrs. Harriman's curiosity was responsible for the visit of her banker husband.

Whitney shrugged. "Perhaps. Perhaps. But the profits are up. I have a balance sheet here— "

"Don't bother. Don't trouble yourself." Harriman's smile distorted his mustache. "Funny thing for a man like Stone to do— lose himself at sea."

"Very strange. But he was shaken. Grievously shaken."

"Oh— true. A tense man. An idealist. A great loss to journalism."

"To the country, Harriman."

"Yes, indeed. The whole country." He paused. "You don't believe, do you, that there's any chance— any remote chance— that he isn't lost— for life?"

It was the hundredth time Whitney had been asked that question— in public and in private, by dowagers at austere functions in Washington Square and by his office boy. He realized that Harriman expected to receive a true answer— and he was ready with the truth as he knew it, although he felt he was answering Mrs. Olive Harriman's curiosity rather than the banker's honest interest.

"I think the *Falcon* went down," he said gravely.

"No hint of anything else?"

"None."

"How did he leave his properties?"

"In trust. In a holding company. For his son— for ninety-nine years. Then for the extant employees of the organization or organizations."

"I see. Don't you think that's a bit suggestive?"

The lawyer walked to the window. He rocked on his feet so that his Prince Albert touched the front and then the back of his knees. He watched the carriages and vans that poured back and forth across Brooklyn Bridge. "Not at all. He expected to return. At least— he expected his son to come back."

"Ah."

"But I've had every possible investigation made. He sailed from Aden in October. There were winds and storms. He went woefully undermanned— a crew of two, I believe. The *Orkney*, bound from Cape Town to Batavia, sighted him, making south under a little sail. That was the last. There was nothing in the way of land south of his position except the Antarctic ice. I'm afraid he's gone, Harriman."

The banker seemed disappointed. "I had hoped— as had my wife— that you might give a few friends— privately, of course— a vestige of optimism."

"I'm sorry." Whitney was impassive at the mention of Harriman's wife— but his recognition of the source of the call was affirmed by it.

"Well— I must go along. Business, you know. Business. It's improving— although 'ninety-seven nearly dumped my cart."

"Please pay my respects to Mrs. Harriman."

"Indeed I shall. And mine to Mrs. Whitney."

They bowed twice.

Mr. Harriman went out on the street. A newsboy recognized him and tipped his hat. He signaled to his coachman and presently drove away toward Wall Street.

Some while later Elihu Whitney appeared on the sidewalk. He stepped into one of the carriages that lined the street. The driver took down the "For hire" sign.

"Mouquin's," the lawyer said.

Time began to mint the bright years. Man's dates turned the century. The tempo of life in America increased. Stephen Stone began to be forgotten and the type on the masthead of the *Record* carried his name in less and less conspicuous sizes. The *Record* bought a paper in Cleveland and one in Chicago. Elihu Whitney's sideburns produced their first streak of gray. Harriman shaved off his mustache. Gas lights went out and electric lights took their place. Telephones spread everywhere. Phonographs played. Langley and Wright began to watch birds.

On the island there was one marked change. The baby that had been brought there in a basket had deserted it. Jack used it now for carrying coal from the pile on shore to McCobb's forge. There was, in fact, no baby any longer — but a person. A very young person.

Henry Stone, at six, had blue eyes and hair the color of a new penny. His skin was dark, like his father's, and, despite a round muscularity, he showed signs of becoming at least as tall as the owner of the now disintegrated *Falcon*. He had an amazing vitality and a constant interest in all the phenomena of life, no matter how common or how inconsequential.

His first step had been a delight to the three men. His fiftieth step had inaugurated their worries.

They were entranced when he had started to talk. And at that time Stephen Stone had put in effect his policy for the child.

Henry was disciplined.

He was taught to read at the age of four, sitting on his father's knee, holding a book, scowling and perspiring in an effort to do as he was told.

He was educated in the matter of independence. He dressed himself. He did his own errands.

Duties were given to him. He fed the chickens and hung up his own clothes.

He was also tutored in the uses of an outdoor life. At five he could swim almost indefinitely in the wire enclosure that

McCobb had made in the sea. His short legs could keep up tirelessly with his father's strides.

Possibly Stephen Stone was impatient to see his system in effect, and perhaps the boy was precocious, for he had advanced in learning to read and write and spell well beyond the place designated for a child of six by common schools. He certainly had gained on all ordinary children of his own age in the matter of his knowledge of the outer world. McCobb had supplemented his father's lessons in games and sports with all the knowledge of trees and flowers, insects and reptiles, fish and birds and animals that he had gained. McCobb had become a competent biologist in six years, with the aid of the books that Stone had brought from America.

Jack, who was devoted to him, contributed little to his wisdom and much to his soul. Jack had the power of consoling him when he had been hurt or frightened and of amusing him when time hung heavy on his small hands.

Time was seldom freighted for him, however. His progress was due largely to the fact that his life became the principal concern of the three men — their entertainment, their escape, their amusement, their pride — and, in different ways, the outlet for what might have been their love.

Stone permitted no great show of affection or friendship. He insisted on justice, prohibited pampering, and developed a code of relationships in which he was master, McCobb was a sort of uncle, and Jack was a privileged retainer.

Henry loved the life. He was born, in any case, to love life and he knew no other existence.

In the morning he would wake with the birds. He would go to the beach, accompanied by Jack, who carried a rifle — in all those years vigilance had not relaxed and there had been occasions to justify it — and swim inside the net. Then he would feed the chickens. After that he would have breakfast with his father and "Mr. McCobb."

When breakfast was finished, lessons began. At six he was reading and using a dictionary for the words he did not know;

he had commenced arithmetic; he was studying geography; he could write quite well; and McCobb was teaching him how to weave baskets and mats and hats and how to make maps out of clay and bookends from boards cut with a scroll saw.

After lunch, for one hour, he rested. Then he was permitted to join in the life of his community. Sometimes he went fishing with Jack. Sometimes he walked along the beach with McCobb and learned about the things that lived there— or into the woods with his father. He volunteered for everything— from washing the clothes to butchering one of the tame zebus.

Often he gave cause for alarm.

There was the momentous day when his wail came from the edge of the stockade on the inside.

"Father! Father!"

Stone ran through the door. His son was standing on something.

"Come here! I got one."

"One what?"

"Snake."

Stone ran. Henry was standing on the end of a stick— the opposite end of which pinioned to earth a venomous serpent.

White-faced, Stone dispatched the reptile. His fear made him angry.

"Don't you know any better than to meddle with a thing like that?"

Henry nodded his head. "I know better. But it was coming after me so I picked up the stick and put it on it. I couldn't hold it down with my hands so I stood on it. Then I couldn't reach it and there weren't any stones or sticks— so I had to get somebody."

"Good Lord."

"It was just starting to slip when you came."

Stone realized that his son's embarrassment and careful explanation was in apology for the fact that he had found it necessary to summon assistance. He did not, at that precise moment, take the trouble to admire the quality.

"After this, if you see a snake, you get out of its way as fast as you can and call someone immediately."

There was the day when Stone himself had carelessly left open the door of the stockade. Henry had wandered out and McCobb had shut the portal. They had not missed the child for what they afterward assumed to be more than an hour.

Jack announced the first sign of the disappearance. "I'm looking for Mr. Henry."

Stone, who was reading on the porch, glanced from his book at his watch.

"He's probably out with McCobb."

"No, sir. Mr. McCobb's in the shop making shoes."

"Then he's around the compound. Henry!" Stone called through the window in the tone parents use the world over to summon their offspring.

No answer.

"You'll find him."

Ten minutes later a grayish Jack returned. "He's gone."

"Gone!" Stone's book dropped.

In a second he was in the yard. He had picked up his rifle. Jack had summoned McCobb. They threw open the gate.

"That way, McCobb. I'll go this. You take it to the beach, Jack."

Jack nodded and flourished the butcher knife that he had snatched from the kitchen table. His expression would have chilled a gorilla.

McCobb paused long enough to call, "Don't worry, Stone. The boy will be all right."

But Stone had already plunged out of sight on the trail to the zebus.

McCobb trotted toward the brook with an anxious face. Stone ran headlong to the corral and found nothing. It was Jack who located the child and set up a wild hallooing. They converged on the beach. Jack was wreathed in smiles.

"He was sitting here on the sand fishing." Jack held up a pole that had been pulled from a bush and to which was tied a long vine. There was neither hook nor bait.

Henry fidgeted.

His father sat down weakly. "You know you should never go out without someone, son."

"How old do I have to be before I can go alone?"

"Fourteen."

"Couldn't I go a little way when I'm seven?"

"No."

McCobb caught his lost breath. "Did you think you'd be able to catch anything with that, Henry?"

The child looked at his tackle. "Nothing very big," he confessed, "but I thought maybe a little teeny, teeny fish would bite the end and I could pull it out before it could let go."

Jack exploded into laughter. Stone postponed his lecture on taking illicit advantage of open gates. They returned to the house.

Sometimes, at night, McCobb and Stone would talk. Often they would sit for long hours in silence — for they had covered long ago most of the subjects that they thought would be of mutual interest. Occasionally, now, their discussions would be of the world and what was taking place there.

"We left at an interesting time," McCobb would say, and Stone would not need to wonder if there were faint and unprotesting regret in his voice. "That fellow Edison was starting things to hum. I don't think the possibilities of electricity were ended with the invention of incandescent lights and power, and whatnot, either."

"Then — there's flying."

"Fiddle-faddle," said Stone, remembering an editorial he had written on the subject.

"Well — you can't overlook balloons."

"I can overlook balloons," Stone would reply. "And I do overlook balloons." Something of his drawing-room manner would return to him. "Let's straighten out the problems of travel on the ground, I say, before we start spinning cobwebs in the sky.

I trust I am progressive — but I also trust a thousand years of civilization are realized before man takes wings."

"I'd like to have a look at the bay on the southeast corner of the island." McCobb always submerged his wonderings about the world they had left with a little forage on his own in the local bush.

"Go ahead. Take the boat."

He would take the boat — if the weather promised to hold — and in some seasons it was absolutely steady — and sail out of the harbor and along the coast.

Then a new McCobb would come into being. He would be master of himself, sailing his own small ship, in his own world, on his own business. He'd smoke and steer and stare.

He had, thus, found the crocodile-ridden swamp at the head of the lake. He had discovered the unnamed birds that were taller than ostriches and laid eggs a foot long and that had extremely violent dispositions.

One day he returned from an absence of forty-eight hours with a cloth bag, which he took to the "shed." He spent some time there and talked to Stone about it that night, after they had shared a bottle of wine to celebrate his homecoming.

"I have a little surprise for you," McCobb said.

"New bird? Because if that's it — I had enough of birds the first time I saw those filthy creatures."

"No." McCobb fished in his pocket and poured a handful of shining metal on the table.

Stone stared at it. "Is it?" he asked finally.

McCobb nodded. "Gold. Pure gold. I found it in those hills north of the lake. In rotten quartz. There's enough on the surface to sink a ship."

Henry bent over the treasure. "Can I have some?"

"May I have some," his father suggested.

"May I?"

"You may have it all, Henry. It's no good to me."

"Unless," Stone suggested, "you want to go into the ornament business. It works easily — and it might be something for

Henry to learn. There's a book about it around here. Benvenuto Cellini and so on."

The Scot stared at the metal. "I wonder if I could do that sort of thing?"

"Why not?"

McCobb developed a new interest that eventually became almost a passion.

The year 1905 they remembered as the year of the hurricane. It came at the turn of the monsoons.

Henry was at his studies when McCobb spoke about it to Stone. "Probably time for it now."

"For what?" Henry asked, glad of an excuse to end his work.

"A change of the prevailing winds," his father said. "Go ahead, now. Seven plus six plus three divided by four is how much?"

Outside the skies were thickening— not rapidly as in a northern thundershower, but slowly, as if more fury was to be reaped for patient effort. The sun went out before the morning "schoolwork" was finished. The sky where it had been was first white, then cream colored, then gray in darkening shades to black.

Leaves withered and scant puffs of air made them wing heavily.

The first lightning was very far away and merely made the beholders guess that they had caught a flash. Soon distant clouds were evanescently silhouetted. Thunder stirred.

Then it was on them. The wind rose like a siren. The rain came slantwise and so rapidly that it collected on slopes, and the ground in the compound seemed to be bouncing with peas from a celestial hopper. It became impossible to talk in anything like an ordinary tone.

Henry was calm. He watched his father's face for his cues. But presently, as the speed and pressure of the gale grew, it became obvious that his father was worried.

Henry bent toward his ear. "It's only wind and rain. They're soft," he shouted.

His father answered with an absent nod.

It grew cold — colder than it had ever been on the island. Jack lighted a fire in the grate, but a separate gust came down the chimney and blew it into the room. A second fire was extinguished by a rush of water.

Henry stared through the window. It was dark outside but he could see the under sides of the nearest trees turned whitely upward in the wind.

The thunder bowled directly overhead. Lightning never stopped but danced from place to place.

The wind increased in pitch and velocity until those who sat in the shaking house believed it could increase no more, and until it became intolerable to their nerves and then it did increase and renew and add to its ferocity.

Henry was least terrified of all.

His father thought that the house would go at any moment. It was unsafe to leave, for huge trees were crashing in the forest and their roots were dragged like brooms across the land. Jack sat and rocked his body. The Scot muttered steadily.

Henry bent near to the Negro and heard him wail, "I wish I was home, home, home!"

When he went to McCobb, the Scot looked at his watch and shouted to him: "You better go to bed. That's where all good little boys and girls should be now."

Henry went finally and sat beside his father on a hassock. The thatch was ripped from the roof in a single blast and water began to dribble into the room.

For six hours the terror was endured and then, abruptly, its last breath whistled over the Indian Ocean and peace was restored.

The men relaxed.

It was early night, and here and there a star briefly appeared. Everyone went outdoors to investigate the damage, but Henry was abstracted. He did not react in his usual way when Jack came running from the zebu pen and said that a man was lying under a tree.

They went, armed, to see. They found a hairy back and a body that had a shape more or less human. But it was not a man. It had a tail and a foxlike head and it was dead.

Stone stared at it. "That's a lemur," he said, at last. "A giant lemur. There were some in prehistoric times. They must be mighty shy— not to have showed themselves in all these years."

Jack frowned. "That's not a man?"

"No, Jack. Not a man."

"Dawgone. That's what I saw the first night we was here. And now I recollect what was funny about that there man. He had a tail."

The minds of McCobb and Stone harked back through time to the first hours of their arrival and they remembered Jack's "man." They exchanged glances. Here was at last the final lifting of the long unspoken thought that perhaps somewhere in the secret places of the island a breed of men lived furtively. They turned over the dead animal and looked at Jack and smiled.

But Henry had received two new ideas, born of the stress of the hurricane. He was scarcely interested in the lemur. He spoke of his ideas when his father came to his bedside before he had fallen asleep.

Henry's blue eyes were wide and intent in the gloom. "Father!"

"Yes, son."

"Isn't this home?"

"Yes, son. It's all the home we have." His silhouette, tall and supple, bent over the bed.

"Then why did Jack say he wished he was home?"

"Oh— did he say that?"

"In the lightning."

"I'll explain all about it tomorrow, son. It's part of your geography lesson."

"Oh."

"Go to sleep."

"Father!"

Patiently now, "Yes, son?"

"What are girls?"

A long pause. A pause so long that it marked the mind of the child. "Girls?"

"Boys and girls. I'm a little boy. What's a girl? Are they little, too?"

Stone realized that they had grown away entirely even from the mention of women. His silence had been the result of his life. But the silence of McCobb and Jack was doubtless in deference to him. "Girls are part of another lesson, son. I'll tell you about them."

"Now?"

"Not now. Go to sleep."

"'Night."

"Good night."

The years on the island passed with unbelievable speed, from the standpoint of retrospect. They mingled and telescoped in a memory of similar days and regular changes of the two seasons. Little things made separate days stand out. They recalled events, but they confused dates.

A day when Henry was observed by his father floating in his boat on the pond-still harbor and looking intently overboard. His father stood on the beach and watched. He wondered what the boy was seeing. And then, suddenly, the water near the boat broke and there emerged a long and terrible arm, a sinuous arm, covered with saucer-shaped suckers and feeling in the unfamiliar air.

Henry regarded the arm with interest but his father paled. "Row, son, row! Come ashore!"

"There's an odd thing down here in the water— "

"I know. Hurry— it's a devilfish."

Henry rowed in obediently although reluctantly and his sweating father saw that the monster followed him nearly to the water's edge.

Was Henry nine, then, or ten?

How old was he when they began to talk in French and German instead of English? Eight for French? Seven?

It was on his twelfth birthday that he showed his father the chalice he had carved from wood and covered with gold leaf. Its shape was handsome, but the horses he had engraved upon it were faintly like the pictures of horses but woefully unlike horses in the flesh.

It was on his twelfth birthday that Stone discussed him with McCobb. Faithful McCobb. He had passed fifty. His eyes were still clear and his muscles firm — but his hair was salted with gray.

"What do you think of the lad, McCobb?"

"He's a grand lad."

"And what are his faults?"

"None," the Scotchman said loyally.

"And what characteristics might become faults in him?"

McCobb drew on his pipe. "That's different. He's independent and fearless. He's idealistic. You can have ideals here in this wilderness but the world would shock them rudely. He's willful and stubborn."

"That's true."

"And I've never seen a lad who had no contact with the lassies. It makes them strange. He's manly enough and he's polite. He'd make friends swiftly in any city — but he's strange. There's a look in his eye — an absent look — that's going to increase, Stephen, when he passes fourteen and begins to feel things he cannot define."

Stone sighed. "I've told him, McCobb — all about women. About women as mothers. And I've recounted their sins. Their shortcomings. Their lack of imagination and their superficiality. I've tried to educate him — prejudice him, perhaps — without lying. He understands."

"But will he understand when he begins to hunger — "

"That hunger," Stone said with a quick anger, "is deceitful."

"Deceitful, maybe — but it's strong, Stephen. It's mightily strong. And here it'll be like wanting the moon. Not even the moon — because you can see that."

"Do you resent my plan, McCobb — after all these years?"

"I do not. He's a fine lad. I was thinking only yesterday that I'd like to start him with the higher mathematics. You'll be well along to making a newspaperman of him, with your exercises and your editorial writing and your discussions of news and policy. But I can make an engineer of him, too, and it'll do him no harm. Jack's taught him to play the banjo — and we might as well combine to make him the cistern of all our knowledge. I'll teach him science."

"You've done very well."

The Scotchman chuckled. "I've done a little. He's learned his botany and his zoology. There isn't a plant on the island he hasn't gathered and we've invented names for the ones we cannot find in the books, as you know. But I made a mistake about not telling him of devilfish — having never seen one in these waters."

"I don't think you should be blamed for that. He should have had the sense to see that it was an unwholesome thing."

McCobb shrugged. "That's a characteristic of him. He has the sense — but his interest is always getting the best of his caution."

Henry came round the house at that moment. He had been spading in the garden. His young shoulders were bare and his skin was Indian color. His hair had darkened a little and it now hung damply over his brow. He wore trousers of soft-tanned leather and shoes not unlike low riding boots. He grinned.

"I got the new bed spaded. I'll plant it this afternoon."

"Good work. You didn't have to finish it today. It was a two-day job."

"You get full of energy," Henry said to his father. "And then — you want to work."

"Even on your birthday."

"Of course. What's the difference?"

"I was going to give you a recess from your studies this afternoon."

"I'd like that."

"And you can choose what you want to do."

Henry sat down on the step and considered. "Well — I'll fix that clock right after lunch. I've had it apart for four days now and every time I put it together there's something left over." He laughed.

McCobb interrupted him. "He won't let me help."

"I'll get it. Then I want to swim. I swam a hundred and six

feet under water yesterday. McCobb measured it. After that — let's go for one of those pumas."

That was when Henry was twelve.

At fourteen or fifteen he sailed the big boat alone in the harbor and sometimes even outside the harbor. He went with his father and helped him build three signal fires — one on each claw of the land that surrounded the bay and one on the top of the mountain. He read about the use of the lasso, at that time, too, and the idea enthralled him.

He made a lariat and practiced throwing it with such intensity that it was difficult to make him study for several weeks. He became proficient in the use of his lasso, and startled his father by announcing that someday he was going to find where the big lemurs lived and rope one of them so that he could bring it home alive.

In those years they had one very long and wet rainy season. They opened a good many of the copper drums that Stone had stored in the cellar. Jack caught a fever that kept him in bed delirious for a long time and once, while Henry was taking care of him, the Negro raved for an hour and more about a girl named Clara.

In those years they moved the garden from the stockade to the broad pampas where the zebus lived in their corral and they worked the ground by setting the steam winch in the middle of the place selected and pulling in the plow and harrow, so that the patch resembled a huge wheel with furrows for spokes. Henry ran the winch and Jack dragged back the implements after each inpull.

Stone was stung by a scorpion and was incapacitated for many days. McCobb filled his room and the shelves in the living room with golden ornaments and statues and vases and bowls that he made in his shop. Henry often helped him work.

In those years Henry's voice broke into sudden bass notes and returned two octaves to its childhood pitch until it finally settled in a rich baritone. Jack taught him to sing parts. Stone forbade the ballads about women. They made brand-new furniture for the house and they developed flower gardens inside the stockade.

Henry grew rapidly — too rapidly, for a while — so that his towering back and spreading shoulders were gaunt and thin. But when he began to fill that frame with sinew it became apparent he would be a majestic man. His boyhood handsomeness took on some of his father's sculptured aquilinity.

They found where the lemurs lived — in the thick forest on the other side of the mountain. They found sapphires in a rusty escarpment of one of the lesser hills.

Henry made a dozen maps of the island and it was he who became fatigued with the familiar terms: "The Island," "The Mountain," and "The Lake."

He changed them to "Stone Island," "McCobb Mountain," and "Jack's Lake."

To him, all the years were divided into happy and fascinating days. The world was his. He was having the romance of a Robinson Crusoe with the equipment that might have been provided by a Jules Verne. He was the modern man and the dawn man. No better life could have been arranged for a boy. None more exciting, none more healthful, none more adventuresome.

Then in 1915, a strange cloud passed over them.

It began with the change of the monsoons. This time they blew almost with hurricane violence, but steadily. Day and night the storm-wracked trees bent and sang. The surf turned the color of canvas and toiled mightily over the reefs beyond the end of Stone Island.

Henry read and studied in his father's dog-eared library.

He counted the hours of the storm and waited patiently for it to abate. There was nothing else to do.

But after the seventy-fifth hour, the rain ceased falling and the wind continued. The vegetation shook itself dry. The sea piled up prodigiously, so that its smash upon the shore could be heard above the gale. The skies cleared a little and illumination came with the hours of dawn.

Henry grew restive. He went finally to his father and shouted that he was going for a walk. His father bade him be careful, and he left.

He went along the more exposed land arm of the bay. He forced his way against the wind — which penetrated even the undergrowth.

He came out on a rocky headland where the sea broke. It moved in lofty, sullen billows. They bent forward, stumbling on their green bases, and wrecked themselves upon the rocks, changing into foam and hurling ragged spray into the wind. The spent waves were sucked back. New waves came.

That spectacle Henry watched with mature composure.

He had an inward desire to throw out his arms and shout back at the surf with all his power, but he controlled it and stood still, watching the unreasoning fury of the sea before and below him.

In a few moments he was drenched with spray.

He tossed back his hair and grinned a personal taunt at the water. He felt exalted. He felt strong.

He stayed for an hour, watching the tumult. Then he was joined by McCobb, who picked his way carefully over the slippery headland and shouted something in his ear that could not be understood and that was vaguely explained by signs.

McCobb, too, felt the majesty of the sight. McCobb at heart was an artist. His northland exterior hid a multitude of appreciations and sensitivities.

They were like two men listening to a great orchestra — each delighting in the fact that his companion also heard and comprehended.

Then, suddenly, Henry felt McCobb's fingers bite into his arm. He looked with surprise at the Scotchman and found that his face was chalky and his arm extended.

The boy's eyes followed the arm. Far out at sea, beyond

the place where the waves individualized themselves, there was a ship.

Henry froze.

McCobb screamed in his ear: "Get your father!"

Henry ran back. He ran like a madman, ignoring the ripping brush and the irregular ground. In his mind's eye was a picture of the ship— a distant, diminutive hulk with bare spars sticking up against the inhospitable horizon.

He burst furiously into the house. "A ship!" His voice clove through the tempest's uproar.

His father read assurance on his face. His father rose gropingly. Into his eyes a fever came and he shook like a leaf. He trotted to the kitchen, plucked Jack's arm, and together they followed Henry.

McCobb was dancing and screaming on the headland. He whirled his arms.

Stone looked. Then he regarded his son, whose soul was in his eyes.

Jack had knelt and folded his hands. He stared into the clouds that scudded overhead and his lips moved in prayer.

The drama on the rocks was horrible in its intensity. Henry found himself frozen, and he could neither think nor move. Stone praised God. Here was a ship at the very hour and year when he had hoped a ship would come. His son was ready for the world. He thought that it would be impossible to light the fires. He reckoned with acid determination upon the chances of the vessel.

It was still far away, and yet it must have sighted the island. It was making slowly toward it— and it could not have made in any other direction. A schooner. One of its masts had been hacked down by the gale. It wallowed heavily— as if it was partly filled with water.

It approached.

McCobb continued to scream and wave his arms. Henry stood still.

The waves visibly lifted it. They could see water washing

over the decks. They could see the laborious rise of the bows and a long rope that had broken loose and stood out horizontally from a mast.

It was two miles away.

One.

They tried to wave it toward the harbor mouth, although all of them knew that direction was impossible.

Stone bruised his son's arms. They saw how far the ship had settled.

Their voices ripped into the air, shrilly. When, at length, they could see the forms of men moving on the bridge, they went mad.

Then a wave came from which the vessel rose only with the utmost difficulty.

They saw a huge hole that had been staved in the hull. Whether the ship had hit a rock, or the mere power of the sea had broken it in, they did not know.

On the next wave the decks were awash.

It was almost near enough so that they could see the expression on the faces of the men.

On the third wave, only the stern rose and the bows were buried.

The masts made an angle with the water.

The stern stood high.

She sank.

McCobb beat his fists upon the rocks until they ran red.

Jack rent his clothes.

Henry wept.

And now, only Stone stood still — as if a judgment had come upon him.

There was no sign of the ship — save that by and by they observed pieces of wreckage and, for a while, what they thought was a man swimming.

Henry ran for his boat. Jack and Stone needed their united efforts to hold him back. Henry's boat would not have been able to round the harbor mouth in the sea that ran there.

As if in satirical compensation the wind died that afternoon and the sun appeared. With its first rays, the four men who sat on the rocky point were able to salvage the first high-tossed bit of wreckage.

It was an oar.

Then came a box in which were four drowned chickens.

A coat.

After that, a broken boat, a life preserver that floated high in the subsiding surf, and a chair.

They struggled with numb endeavor to reap these precious and yet melancholy items from the waves.

Bits of the ship itself drifted shoreward. Late in the afternoon their heap of debris was augmented by a score of things — wooden bowls from the galley, spars, planks, a straw cover from a bottle of wine, and a pillow.

They saved everything as it came in, and all that time they had not spoken to each other.

At last Stone, wading on the rocks, picked up a cupboard and he perceived that the inside was lined with newspaper, tacked on shelves.

The sight of that newsprint devastated him.

He hugged the box to his person. He pulled the tacks with his nails, heedless of the pain. He rolled the wet paper with the utmost care and, when he saw that his find had not been noticed by the others, he hurried secretly back to the house.

The first words he saw inflamed his mind. He could not help his selfishness and fanatic greed for news.

GERMANS ADVANCE ALONG MARNE SECTOR.

That is what he had read.

As he went to the house his mind reeled. Germans advance. There was a war up there in the world. A war that involved Germany.

He locked himself in his room. He spread the wet pages with agonizing care and as he worked his eyes gleaned fragments. Woodrow Wilson was President of the United States.

England was at war with Germany. Also France. The name of Russia appeared as a combatant.

Finally, the papers were spread and he focused his eyes. He read.

He forgot that salvation had missed them by a terrible margin — a margin at once minute and gigantic.

He forgot his son and McCobb and Jack.

He became for a little while the man he had been — the man of the world, the political power. And he became a student of the new world. They were moving troops through Paris in omnibuses and taxicabs? What were taxicabs? The *Stutram* had radioed for help. What was radioing? The British line was holding well and Paris would be saved.

Paris.

Ah, God, Paris.

The curves of the Seine and the cold gray of Notre Dame. The wide passage of the Boulevard Montparnasse past the place where he had lived when he studied there. The still dark places of the Bois and the songs and the wine and the lights and the music.

German guns were belching and French blood was making a red mud of Flanders fields but Paris would be saved.

Paris!

On the headland, wading in the seaweed and sliding on the rocks over which water gushed, three men hunted for souvenirs of their Gethsemane.

Henry rubbed shoulders with McCobb. The Scotchman was holding a shoe.

"Somebody's," he said, in a world where "somebody" was a word seldom used.

The expression was forlorn, so hopeless and woebegone, that Henry's spirit turned in its tracks.

He grinned.

"We can make better shoes than that."

The sentence rallied the Scot. His eyes lighted and on his tough face there came a smile both radiant and calm.

"Let's go back to see your father," he suggested. "There's no virtue in this salvage and more'll wash up on the sand down the point."

"Right. Come on, Jack."

The Negro flashed his teeth from habit. "Yes, Mr. Henry."

They moved away from the place in slow file, heartened by an emotional chemistry that the indomitability of Henry's eyes had started.

Thrice they knocked at the locked door of the bedroom before reluctant motion responded.

Stone came out and never did he look more like the substance of his name. His granite face was fixed. He recognized them as if they were not people, but far-fetched theories.

"There's a war," he whispered.

McCobb had seen madness and he was much frightened, but Henry, who had never seen it, laughed.

"War? What are you talking about, father?"

Vacantly, Stone stared. "I found a newspaper in that stuff— that floated— ashore. I've been reading it."

"That's fine, father! It must have been great!"

"It was hideous."

"What do you mean?"

"I— " He walked into the center of the living room, where the handmade furniture was arranged between shelves of books and corpulent cupboards, where McCobb's golden handiwork gleamed and where in the shadows were the stuffed birds and animals Henry had collected. "I— "

McCobb pulled out a chair. "Sit down, Stephen. You're overwrought. Jack— bring a drink of whisky."

Stone swallowed the spirits. He began to talk. "I've read it all. It will be dry soon— and then the rest of you can have it. It taught me— something. It taught me a great deal. It taught me that my coming here— was criminal. It was criminal to you and to Jack— but I had discounted that. It was criminal to my son— but I had an alibi for that.

"It was criminal to myself."

Henry gave back the words he had been told so often. "Why— father— you know it was an accident. The ship was in bad shape and you needed water and you smashed up here— and why blame yourself?"

"It— " Stone began and McCobb, terrified lest the boy who was so nearly a man be told the truth, held up his finger and spoke heartily.

"You couldn't help it. It's nothing."

Stone avoided the eyes of his son. They were very bright and speculative at that instant. He cleared his throat. "But it's my fault. I took too great a risk. And I stranded all of us here."

"Fiddlesticks!" said McCobb.

"You are plumb out of your haid," Jack said.

"When they need me," Stone continued. "When they need me. They need me in America today. They'll need me more tomorrow, if I am any reader of signs. I had a duty greater than any other and I ran away from it into this cloying wonderland. I'm a fool!"

"Stephen— "

"Father— "

"A fool, gentlemen."

Stone stalked from the room. No one followed him for several minutes and then Jack stepped from the shadows. "I think I'll just run along behind to see that everything's all right."

McCobb nodded. "Go ahead, Jack. Thanks. And take this." He held out a revolver. Jack stuck the gun in his belt. It pulled his trousers tight enough to reveal in relief the blade and handle of a butcher knife secreted along his thigh.

Silence descended in the house.

McCobb poured himself a drink from the whiskey bottle.

Henry stared at his feet. His face was covered with a fine, golden down. His chin was like his father's. His hands were lean and powerful. He stroked the down.

"Of course," he said softly to McCobb, "I've always known it wasn't— an accident."

McCobb dropped his glass.

"Steady there, son," the Scot murmured.

"I don't mind— much."

McCobb began the speech to which Henry had long been accustomed: "It was a bad night— "

Henry interrupted, in a low, forceful voice: "I don't mind a great deal. At first— it was just a feeling. When I was little I experienced it. No one ever talked about how we got here. No one ever talked about why the voyage was made. That wasn't natural. So I just felt that our shipwreck was intentional.

"But gradually"— Henry's eyes expanded as he spoke— "I began to think. You taught me about engines and about engineering. I looked at the wreck down on the beach. I dove around it. The propeller had snapped. That, of course, wouldn't happen under accidental conditions— would it?"

The Scot drank again. This recital of the powerful blond youth who sat idly in the chair was more harrowing to him, in a way, than the afternoon's disaster.

He said nothing.

"I don't mind. I know father did it."

"Henry, my lad— "

"Don't worry. I'll never accuse him of it. He'll never guess that I know."

"Good man!"

"Or that I know why."

McCobb's scalp prickled. "Why?" he repeated stupidly.

"Why. It was— on account of a woman." He did not raise his eyes to ask for confirmation. Instead he rose and poured McCobb's third drink, which he took from limp hands, back into the bottle.

"Let us take a walk, too," he said, with a smile that was poignant and charming and that McCobb always accounted afterward as a sort of miracle.

It was the second time that day that Henry had saved McCobb from intolerable emotions.

They went out into the sunlight together.

It was 1917.

The table in the "living room" of the island house was exquisitely set. A strange function was taking place.

Separated by spotless napery and beautiful silver, by white china and crystal glasses brimming with wine, were Stephen Stone and his son. Their ordinary habiliments of heavy cloth and soft-tanned rawhide were missing. Instead, they wore dinner clothes. Dinner clothes of the late nineteenth century — Stephen's fitting perfectly, and Henry's somewhat too small for his frame — but dinner clothes with satin lapels, and boiled shirts.

Behind them, as they commenced to eat their green turtle soup, Jack stood at rigid attention and there was no sign of amusement on his face.

Stone touched his napkin to his lips and spoke to his son. "They tell me, Mr. Stone, that Bryan's championship of bimetallism will sweep the country."

Henry lifted his eyebrows with elegant hauteur. "I've read his speeches. A cheap and dangerous demagogue. Something about 'crucifixion on a cross of gold.' Well — if gold is too heavy a burden for the people to carry about, they'll find that free silver will make their pockets light enough."

"William Jennings Bryan is a menace — " Stephen Stone began, after laughing politely at Henry's witticism. "A decided menace." He interrupted himself. "Henry — that's not the way to hold a wine goblet. Like this."

Henry followed his father's instructions. "Am I right, now?"

"That's better. Now. I'm the Ambassador from Spain. You have just criticized Spanish actions in Cuba and you are unfortunately seated beside me at a dinner given by Mrs. Astor. I am a little bit— perhaps, guardedly, a great deal— perturbed at this unhappy accident. I am thinking of something definitely unpleasant to say about your newspaper. Proceed."

Henry flashed upon his father a winning and wholly artificial smile. "My dear Mr. Ambassador— "

"My dear Ambassador Chinito— "

"My dear Ambassador Chinito— this is luck. I've been wanting to meet and talk with you for months. The information we receive at my office relative to Spanish policy is at best vague and uncertain, and this opportunity to discuss it with a master of statecraft is handsome Providence indeed."

Stephen Stone smiled. "A little flowery. But good. Now. I am — oh— Jack— remove the soup. The serving plates. I am— "

The conversation continued endlessly. The meal lasted two hours. It was a new function on Stone Island. A new course in Stephen Stone's instruction of his son. He had planned it long, long ago. He had brought the necessary adjuncts. He was training Henry for his social life, training him how to be a perfect guest, a polished conversationalist, and diplomatically quick-thinking— all in the manner and according to the best traditions of a period that was already twenty years old.

He taught him how to dress— although when he had ordered the clothes, in London, in 1897, he had not guessed his son would attain such stature. He taught him etiquette, and how to dine and what to order, and how to order from a waiter in Delmonico's and from a waiter in Jack's and what to do in London and Paris and Vienna and where to go. He taught him how to behave in a men's club and in a bank and in the box of an opera.

He taught him all the important trifles and they lived through a thousand scenes and situations, for one night each week was designated to represent some sort of function. Invitations were sent and Henry answered them. The table was set meticulously and Stephen Stone portrayed the various guests— sometimes playing three or four roles at once.

At the same time, he intensified his courses in politics and the newspaper business. He made Henry write a complete edition of a newspaper for Stone Island every two weeks. He discussed with his son the politics of his day — for there was no other material open to their contemplation. He taught the mechanics of the business, the functions of the various departments, the financing and the methods of development.

He educated his son to be a public speaker, and with Jack and McCobb for his audience, Henry frequently stood on the front porch, vines, trees, and gaudy birds behind him, the sea before, and waxed eloquent on the administration of a proper government, or the fallacies of the Populists, or the trend of policies in the State Department. Sometimes, for variety, he and his father had a debate. McCobb, who rarely joined in these intellectual and social pastimes, was instructed to act as chairman or referee in such cases.

Henry addressed an imaginary Senate Committee on the freedom of the press. He ranted endlessly about Bryan. He raked over the ancient scandals of the Tweed Ring.

He also talked with dowagers in imaginary carriages. Dowagers — and they were always stuffy and frigid — were the only women who invaded this educational policy, and their invasion was rare. He rode in street cars under his father's tutelage. He walked on Fifth Avenue on Easter Day. He listened to sermons and sang hymns — although Stone was himself an agnostic.

A great, vicarious world expanded before him, amplified by poor drawings in books and by his father's excellent descriptions. In that world one thing was paramount: Ideals.

Stephen Stone made them the foundation of all else.

Never lie.

Never cheat.

Be honest.

Be forthright (but tactful).

Stick to your party but hold your country above it.

Be a gentleman (a thousand times that!).

Be a good sport.

Be tolerant (except of certain evils).

Be moderate. Drink moderately. Smoke moderately.

Keep informed.

Sleep eight hours a day and work twelve.

Never, never, never, never believe a woman.

Women are ruin. Love is a myth. Marry when you are over forty-five and marry someone you do not love.

Love is ruin.

Be, above all, fearless.

The precepts were banged out on the table with a fist. They were infiltrated through all their discussions. Henry was shown up flagrantly for the slightest lapse from them.

This was Stephen Stone's reaction to the numb days that had followed the sinking of the ship off the headlands. He had stayed away from the house all night — with Jack in the bush nearby — and he had come back changed. The gaiety that had grown in him vanished. He applied all his energy now to the training of his son.

And Henry slowly lost human contact with his father. He obeyed. He even respected. He worked like a slave. But a rift grew between them. McCobb thought that it was an unconscious breach caused by Henry's unspoken resentment of the fact that his father had stranded him — probably for life — on the island.

It was not.

It grew because the two men were fundamentally different. There was something fanatical, puritanic, masochistic, and sadistic in Stephen Stone. Henry was broad-minded by nature, and generous.

If Henry had been the man whose wife had run away — he might have forgiven her. If Stephen Stone had been the individual whose father deliberately stranded him on an island, he would have eaten out his heart with secret malice and thwarted ambition. The strength of the two men lay in different sinews of the soul.

It was May and 1921.

Stone sat bitterly in the house. Henry had been gone for three days in the sailboat. Stone was bitter because he himself had planned that his son should be independent and go where he pleased when he pleased — and because he found that such journeys occasioned him only worry and loneliness.

He stamped on the floor with a cane that hung on the arm of a chair.

Jack looked from the kitchen. "Yes, boss?"

"Bring me a glass of that port."

"Yes, boss."

When Jack came with the glass on the tray, Stone said: "How much have we left?"

"Of this port?"

"Of this port."

"About a barrel."

"Well — next time I ask for port, bring me some of that stuff we made ourselves. It's not bad."

"No, boss."

"And you get back to your cooking."

McCobb entered from the compound. He was carrying a brace of ducks.

"Nice ones, eh?" He held them up.

Stone did not look at the ducks. He banged irritably on the floor. "It's as quiet around here as the inside of a tomb."

McCobb nodded. "You'd get over that gout quicker, I think, if you were careful with the wine."

"Hell!" Stone seldom used even that initial word of profanity. "Wine! Who wouldn't drink wine? Why the devil doesn't that young whipper-snapper come back here?"

"He'll be in soon," McCobb said. He did not mention his own worries — worries he always felt when Henry traveled alone. He passed behind Stone's back and looked at him almost pityingly. Stone was growing old — and he did not know it. Someday — the mirror would tell him irrefutably.

McCobb was growing old, too. He was years older than Stone, but life had not told so heavily upon him. He had an oaken constitution and a valiant heart. He was ready for the years.

A shrill whistle floated up from the bay. Stone jumped onto his feet and scarcely noticed his gout. He hobbled to the door.

"There he is, damn it!"

McCobb was at his side. They waited impatiently while Henry made fast his boat and came up the road.

He swung along with a prodigious stride. He was a full six feet two inches, now. He weighed a hundred and ninety pounds. His hair was bronze, his eyes turquoise, his skin mahogany. He was a magnificent man. When he laughed his voice poured from deep and resonant lungs.

As he strode through the gate they saw that he had a sack on his shoulders and there was motion inside the sack. He took the front steps at a jump.

"Hello, father. How's the foot?"

"Better, son. Better."

"McCobb! Glad to see you." He dropped the bag, which squirmed. He took the hands of the two men.

"We've missed you," McCobb said.

Henry laughed again. "I've been all over. Put in at the bay north of Jack's Lake. Carried that canoe over to the lake and took myself a paddle."

He walked into the house, the men beside him.

"How was it?" Stephen Stone asked the question.

"Marvelous. Plenty of crocodiles, but they don't bother the boat. Wouldn't like to upset, though." A squeal came from the porch and Henry went out to collect the bag. "I caught a pair of those little peccaries or whatever they are. Hey, Jack!"

The door to the kitchen flew open. "I was coming. I had the lids off the stove and the potatoes in my lap."

"Here's a pair of pigs. We'll breed them for a steady supply of pork."

"Mmm-*mmm*," Jack said. He picked up the bag and looked back. "Glad to see you home, Mr. Henry."

"Thanks."

Stephen Stone sipped his wine. "Well? What else happened?"

"Nothing. I worked on that cabin I'm building at the head of the lake. It's going to be a dandy little spot. Then I'm going to study the geology of the island. I have it all doped out — "

"We had, too, before you were old enough to talk."

"It's volcanic — and the remnant of a continent — isn't it?"

Stone nodded. "There used to be a continent that ran from Africa all the way to India. The lemurs were evolved on it. Madagascar is about the only part of it left."

"That's what I thought. McCobb Mountain is the highest point remaining — and it's part of the rim of a volcano. Jack's Lake is in the crater. And, by the way, there are hot springs up at the head of the lake. They spout out of a row of mud dunes. All colors of mud. Nothing growing. Some are sulphurous and some are salty."

The Scotchman chuckled. "We ought to take your father's gout there and establish a spa."

"The devil with my gout. What else, Henry?"

"Something I want you to see."

The man with the cane laughed. "I knew it! I knew it when you whistled. Well, sir?"

"Ruins."

"Good Lord!"

"Buried in the jungle. I came on them while I was chasing those pigs. Big ruins. Temples, I should think — all made of stone and covered with carving. A language — it looks a little bit like Sanskrit — but I'm not sure. They must have been very beautiful, once, but they're old as time, now. And they've been under water."

"What?"

"Fossilized barnacles and things inside the rooms."

"Are there rooms?"

"You bet there are rooms. Scores of rooms. Big rooms. Carved gods and altars and more decoration than you ever dreamed of." He turned toward McCobb. "We won't have to dig our gold out of the rocks, now. There are tons of it there. And stones. All kinds." He thrust his hand in his pocket and produced two rubies as large as the ball of his thumb. They had been rolled and polished into perfect spheres.

The stones passed from hand to hand. "Silver and other metals. They did a fine job, those people, whoever they were. And they must have left in a hurry, because their things are all over the place. Sand mixed with them. Shells. But they're there, nevertheless."

McCobb clicked the rubies together in the palm of his hand.

"Funny."

Henry shook his head. "Very funny. I wouldn't be surprised if it was the temporary sinking of their temple under the sea that brought them to an end."

"How long ago did you think — ?"

The young man shrugged. "I can't guess. We'll try to figure it out when we go there — but it must be old. Older than Egypt, I should imagine. Older than anything you've told me about."

"The lemur continent went down," Stone said pensively, "in the ages before man appeared."

"Then he's been on the island recently," Henry smiled. "Say in the last twenty-five thousand years. Or maybe even in the last ten. Which — in a manner of speaking — is only yesterday."

November 3, 1923.

Stephen Stone wrote the date in his diary. He wrote it slowly and carefully and his hand was not quite steady. Then he continued:

"It was twenty-five years ago today that we landed on Stone Island. A quarter of a century. Tonight we are having a banquet to 'celebrate,' but our celebration is rather a brave defense than a jubilee.

"Except for the single ship that foundered off our shores, not so much as a gull or a drifting branch has come to us from the world beyond. We might as well be upon another planet with the infinite reaches of the ether between ourselves and those regions that once we called our home. The last statement cannot apply to Henry, whose only home has been the island, although I catch him sometimes in poses of rumination that suggest to me he is not altogether without a dim sentiment for the land from which he came and an inarticulate desire to be there.

"Consciously, however, he seems to prefer the island and has often assured me that he would rather live and die here than to mingle with the society and participate in the enterprises for which I have fitted him to the best of my ability.

"It is never my practice, of course, to admit that he will be prisoner here for life and I keep asserting that with the developments in ocean travel that have doubtless been made and the interest in exploration bound to rise, it is sure that a vessel will one day reach this place. My doubt can only be entered here.

"Horrible thoughts sometimes assail me. A hundred times I have read the portions of the newspaper that came to us with the ill-fated ship and I have thought about the war in progress then. The fact that no one and nothing passes here makes me wonder if the war did not increase to such proportions that it virtually destroyed civilization.

"I imagine sometimes all ships destroyed, all commerce ended, and the people in America reduced to the pioneer state. Or, perhaps, some dreadful weapon has decimated the populations of the world.

"A catastrophe that would blot out mankind, even, might take place unbeknownst to us. Thus, in years, I have commenced to understand the dullness of the isolation that I, in a fit of frenzy and despair, contrived.

"And because that doom was forged by the weak willfulness of a woman, I have redoubled my tutelage of Henry in the subject. Yearly, the idea of woman grows more detestable to me, and in it I repose all my apologia pro vita mea.

"Of manners, people, custom, science, and art, we have very little to add to Henry's store. We have given him our all, searching our minds through the long days for any fragment of truth or wisdom that would be of value to him. He is, I think, a man cultured and disciplined far above any I ever met in my life, and although his manner is generally light and affable, it is but the bright garment with which a pleasant disposition conceals a stern mind.

"We have managed almost annually to invent a new form of entertainment and new interests for him and ourselves. At first these were uncomplicated and simple tasks. The domestication of the zebu-oxen, the establishment of ample vegetable gardens, the building of our now luxurious flower gardens, horticultural experiments with the local flora, the collection and classification of all living things on the island— even, at the last, to a study of microscopic life.

"As time passed, however, these interests became broader. Henry, who has a remarkable physique, passed through a stage of physical exercise and development. McCobb taught him to box and I to fence when he was a child. He became a proficient swimmer and I daresay his prowess in that direction would astonish any of his 'civilized' contemporaries.

"When he was sixteen and until he was twenty-four his studies enveloped him. I believe he has read every one of the books in my library.

"In the past two years he has lived away from the compound a good deal of the time, studying the ruins that he discovered, and his archeological conclusions are very fascinating to him. With the help of my library he has more or less identified the people who built the temples as the offshoot of a very early race— possibly of the Atlanteans, but more probably the descendants of the inhabitants of a great continent in the south Pacific that he predicates from a reading of their inscriptions.

"He is engaged now in writing a book, about the people, and I have seen a few chapters that I find remarkable both for their clarity of style and for the vividness with which he is able to create a background from his reading, a background so lucid that it makes all his deductions most plausible. He informs me that he will seal the book — which contains his full studies of the ancient language — in one of my copper drums so that it will be available long after his living testimony is not.

"Jack's hair has suddenly turned white. I find my own is graying. McCobb is not as alert and agile as he used to be. We are growing old.

"I wonder who will be first?"

Henry sat beside McCobb on the top of the mountain that bore the Scotchman's name. McCobb smoked and Henry ate an apple. They had had apples for twenty years.

The tropical sun beat upon them. It sparkled over the waters of Jack's Lake. It glinted on the tower of a temple far away. Henry had cleared the vegetation around the best preserved portion of the ruins and the result was that a single minaret could be seen from any high spot on the island.

They could see, to the north, the tiny dot that was Jack on the harbor, fishing.

McCobb squinted his eyes so that a hundred wrinkles came at their corners.

"I asked you up here with me, son, because I wanted to talk with you."

"Yes? What about?"

"About yourself."

"Me?"

The old Scotchman nodded. "About you. Yesterday I thought I'd gather some clams for chowder for dinner, so I went down to the outside beach on the west headland."

Henry flushed, but he said nothing.

"There was somebody sitting there," the Scotchman said, trying with a heavy hand to be impersonal, "who was crying. I could hear him from where I was. He was looking over the sea and sobbing. Then he threw out his arms and reached — as if he was reaching for something out there toward the west. Then he beat his chest."

Henry threw a stone over the cliff and the sound of its landing came to them before McCobb continued.

"Finally he laughed. It wasn't a nice laugh to hear. He laughed a long time. Then he jumped into the water and swam and swam and swam. Out where there are sharks. Out where there are devilfish. He swam until an old man with failing eyes, maybe, could see him no more. Then it was the old man's turn to sit down and cry."

Silence.

"I thought you weren't coming back."

"So did I," Henry said.

"But you turned and came in. I saw that, too. So I asked you up here."

Henry looked at the Scot. His face was hard. "I was bored, McCobb. Couldn't stand it."

"I know."

"Would it matter so much if the sharks got me?"

"Well— let's see. It would matter to your dad, of course."

"He doesn't deserve— "

"All right. All right. I don't defend him. But— it would matter to Jack. And to me."

"I'm sorry, McCobb."

"Oh— that's nothing. It's all right. But I had in my mind another person. Yourself. It would matter to you, Henry. A great deal."

"Not as much as you'd think."

"No?"

Henry leaned back on his elbow and squinted at the glittering panorama. "I'm a loss, McCobb. I'm nothing. I'm like a clock— a marvelous clock— that someone spends a lifetime to make and then puts in a grave. I can only tell time to the worms and the worms can't profit by it. My chimes are for stones. The earth holds in my ticking."

"Is that the truth indeed?" McCobb chuckled. "And suppose somebody digs up the clock. What then? You know, laddie, your father is right. Every year that passes adds to the chance that somebody will come past this place. They'll run out of land to explore someday and then they'll start on the sea and cover every square mile to be sure they've missed nothing. They'll cover the surface and drag the bottom.

"And they'll find Stone Island. They'll see McCobb Mountain. We'll touch off this pile of brush" — he gestured toward the heap of wood that had been kept in perennial readiness — "and they'll take us back. Think, Henry. You've never seen even a town — let alone a city. You've never seen a horse. Or a cable car. Or the steam engines that pull the railroads. Or the great bridges on the rivers. Or the steamships. Or a woman."

Henry stirred. "No. Or a woman."

"Never seen a woman," McCobb whispered.

"I'm not sure that I want to."

The words struck McCobb's heart forcibly. Never seen a woman. He knew what women would say when they saw Henry. And he was searching frantically for a reason to tie the young man to his calm life, to give him strength and hope. He dared to trespass on Stone's unchanging sermon.

"Did it ever occur to you, laddie, that your father might be mistaken about women?"

"What do you mean?" Henry spoke breathlessly.

McCobb was frightened. "Nothing much, lad. Nothing much. But it's possible that your father's a bit warped on the subject. Not all women might be bad."

"I don't believe it."

"Think it over. They're the same flesh as yourself. They have the same emotions. They have different minds, it's true — but there are women who don't cost a man his soul. Many."

"Is that true, McCobb?"

"'Tis true. But you'll not tell your father I've said it?"

"I won't tell him."

"Thanks, lad."

Henry stood. "That makes a difference in my life, McCobb. A difference you'll never understand. I've been thinking about women so much that I've been sure they'd ruin me the minute

I got back to land — if I ever did. I found that I would pay no attention to father's teachings. I was sure I would be lost — as he had been. I don't know why. He said their spell was destruction — and I've never seen them — but somehow — I could know something about that spell."

"I've no doubt."

"Look." Henry suddenly reddened. He stuffed his hand into his shirt and from his bosom drew a tiny figure that had hung round his neck on a delicate chain. It was the figure, presumably, of a nude woman.

McCobb looked at it. He did not laugh. He said soberly: "I'll make you one, Henry. I'll make you one like a living woman."

"I didn't do it right," Henry said slowly. "I know. But father tore all the pictures from the books. Even the medical books."

"Let's go back, son."

Henry stretched himself. "I feel — changed, McCobb. Different. Thanks."

"Don't mention it."

For a long time after that Henry did not swim away from shore and he did not weep on the beach. He was gay again and even his father, who was slowly becoming estranged from everyone, noticed the difference. He attributed it to resignation.

chapter
EIGHT

Spring and 1929.

That spring marked the next to the last change in the tempers of the islanders. The one that followed it was final. Henry was a man, then — although his life had been such that he looked five years younger than his actual age. At his father's insistence he had grown a heavy, bronzed mustache that covered his lips and gave him an attribute of years that only emphasized his youthfulness.

The event that postulated the changes in the men occurred during the shift of the monsoons — the time that had punctuated nearly all their mental permutations.

It was a dramatic happening.

An incredible happening.

The monsoon had shifted with an unusual gentleness. There had been the ordinary rains, the regular winds, and the steady flow of gray clouds, but each particular of the phenomenon had been of low degree.

Then the weather had settled. For two weeks they had enjoyed sun and calm.

After that, however, the winds returned. They were forceful winds in comparison to a sea breeze or a down-draft from a mountain range, but they were less than gales. This meteorological variety interested the men. The new winds blew for two days and stopped. The sun shone.

And then, again, came an abrupt alteration. On the 26th of April there was a squall and a lowering of the skies. The day darkened with sunset and the next dawn was black and stormy.

Jack went out on the harbor to fish and gave up.

"My boat blew around like a feather," he reported when he returned to the house.

Stone grunted and sipped his perpetual wine.

McCobb came in from the shop where he had been working. "It's blowing hard," he said.

"Where's Henry?" Stone asked.

"He'll be in. He was helping me."

The window-frames rattled and a door slammed. Stone fidgeted in his chair and growled at the elements.

His son appeared. "This is a fine monsoon. It finished its annual volume of business twice and now it's started in for the third time."

"How's the glass?"

"Falling again."

"Did you fix the pig pen?"

Henry nodded. "Jack did."

"Well— you better look at it. Remember the last time. The pigs got out and bit the goats. The goats butted a hole in their corral— "

"I know, father. It's all fixed. The pig pen won't blow over again."

"Have a glass of wine?"

"No, thanks."

"Keep the fever out of your bones."

Henry looked at his father. The eagle's profile was still bold in old age but around the mouth were lines like scars and the mouth itself trembled sometimes with impotence and indecision. "Keep the fever out," he said cheerfully, "and bring the gout in. You're not well, father. I've noticed that you get out of breath often. You ought to take it easy."

"Take it easy! That's a worthy axiom! In all my life I never took it easy. I— what's that?"

"What?"

A single pulsation had reached Stone's ears. An almost whispered sound, muffled and wind-torn. A sound like the hammering of a woodpecker on a pulpy log. A remote drumming.

"I heard something. But it's gone. Tree in the wind, I guess. Now— about this taking it easy business— "

Henry held up his hand. He, too, had heard the sound. He went to the window and looked out. The low clouds raced perpetually overhead, like newsprint running through celestial presses. Trees bent to the gale.

"Funny," Henry murmured.

On Stone's face was an expression of perplexity, of partial memory, or groping.

Then the sound came so that both could hear it and it was a sound that did not stop. A soft purring sound that issued from outdoors.

Henry was struck by a thought. A blinding thought. He rushed to the door and out on the porch. His father was behind him. He stared over the portion of the sea that was visible, but he could discover nothing save the rising and falling water. Jack ran from the kitchen— by then, the noise had permeated everything. Its intensity was increasing. Behind Jack came McCobb.

And McCobb spoke: "It's an engine!"

"Great God!" Henry said.

"On the sea somewhere— " McCobb continued.

Then Jack said, "There it is. It's— "

"Where?"

"There!" Jack pointed not out on the water but up in the air.

They ran from the porch into the compound. They saw. From out of the lowering southwest a thing sped through the air. It was a speck at first, but it rushed toward them at an incredible speed. Probably all of them considered it as a gigantic and hideous bird for a fraction of a second. They watched with motionless attention.

Stone spoke. "Man," he said softly, "man— has learned to fly. It's an aerial ship. With an engine."

The plane came nearer. It was flying below the clouds and directly toward the island.

They did not repeat the scene they had made when the ship approached their shore. The thing happened too quickly. It was too incredible, too monstrous, too inconceivably remote from their wildest dreams.

They made observations barely loud enough to be heard by themselves. The wind pressed upon them. The sound of the motor overhead became an enthralling roar.

"It's on wings that are stiff," Stone murmured.

"There may be no men in it," McCobb said.

"They'll be here in a few seconds," Henry thought.

Only Jack was silent. He had thrown himself on the ground. His numb mind identified the plane with an angel of the Lord.

It flashed over the island. The shining body was silver. The wings were black. The nose was crimson. There were letters marked along the fuselage and the word "Promise," which they realized later was the name of the ship.

"It's turning!" Henry bawled, suddenly.

It did turn. It banked steeply, swung around in the gale, and came back across them. This time, through glass windows, they saw two down-peering men.

One of them lifted his arm and waved.

The sound of the thing was intolerable. Its size was enormous.

McCobb threw himself in an attitude of supplication. Henry, seeing it, did likewise. Stone waved back toward the miracle that had come in the storm.

The plane zoomed up into the teeth of the gale and swept back a second time. Then they saw the men again and the one at the window first clasped his hands together and shook them. After that he nodded vigorously and then pointed toward the east. The last thing they saw was his friendly wave. The plane turned with the wind again and roared away from the storm. Its sound died rapidly.

From the ground Henry rose. He helped McCobb to his feet.
Together they raised Jack.

Stone motioned them toward the house.

When they were inside, Stone fell upon his knees with his face over the seat of his chair.

"Oh, God," he said in a trembling voice, "if there is a God, speed these men back to— other men. Put wisdom in their minds so they will understand our dire distress and let them bring rescue to us. Forgive us our debts— "

He choked.

In the plane one of the aviators stared at the fast vanishing island. His eyes were wide with wonder. He moved through the tiny cabin and stared at an immense map pasted on a table. A dotted line ran across an empty sea. He added a few dots, after a moment of calculation, and he drew in an island in the shape of a sting ray where before had been unmarked blue.

Then he sat down beside the man at the controls.

"That's something, Chuck."

"My God, yes."

Both of them shouted— the cabin was dizzy with din.

"Those poor devils may have been there for years."

"Must have been. Did you see the house?"

"Yeah. And their boat was on the beach— what was left of it."

"We'll send somebody back from Hobart."

"If we get there ourselves."

"Nuts."

They flew on. It became afternoon and night. Light shone on their instruments. The wind increased. They sat side by side, grim, taut, listening.

In the night there was a break in the sound of the engine and they exchanged terrified glances . . .

"It had wheels on the bottom." They were sitting at the dinner table, drunk with excitement.

"I saw them."

"It must run along the ground until it gathers momentum and then rush into the air."

"It was driven by a screw— like a ship." McCobb's eyes danced. "Man, what a craft!"

"That there engine," Jack said over their shoulders, "sure did rattle."

They laughed too loudly.

"They must have an immense cruising range. It's fully two thousand miles to anything."

"And speed!"

Henry's reminder silenced them.

Stone drew on the tablecloth with a knife and said at last, "How much, Henry? How much, McCobb?"

The engineer considered aloud: "Well— she came by with the wind— going at double the speed of the clouds, or more. When she bucked the wind— tacked square into it— she must have gone as fast as any locomotive. I should hate to guess— but I wouldn't be surprised if in still air she could do— a hundred miles an hour. Maybe a hundred and fifty."

"Great Jehovah!"

Henry became hysterical with laughter. They pounded his back and gave him a drink.

"Let's see," he said finally. "Ten hours— say, twelve hours to the mainland."

"Twelve hours. Why— they'll be landing soon, then. In a few minutes."

Stone nodded. "And the cables will begin to hum. The world will be told. They'll telegraph it all over the United States. My own *Record* will come out tomorrow morning with the news of castaways. A new island. They could certainly see down here well enough— although they went by so fast that they probably missed a good many of the details."

There was a little silence. Henry had the courage to voice the thought so far unspoken.

"I presume that those things do — have accidents — once in a while."

If they had known the hazards of a long transoceanic flight, they would not have been so jubilant.

There was an interval of deeper stillness. McCobb broke it: "They looked as if they knew their business."

Everyone leaped avidly upon that thought. "They were confident!"

"They smiled," Henry said, in defiance of his fear. "They clasped hands and waved and pointed. They understood what we needed, all right."

"Maybe they'll send one of them back for us," McCobb hazarded.

"One of them there airships?" Jack asked nervously.

"Sure. Why not?"

"No, sir. No, siree! I'm a-going to wait for a boat. I don't want to go fooling around among the birds. Not me."

An uproar of laughter in which Jack joined.

"How fast do you suppose their ships can go?"

The use of "they" to mean all the other people in the world was pathetic — but the islanders did not realize that.

"Maybe twenty knots," McCobb guessed. He figured with a pencil on the tablecloth while everyone bent forward. "Twenty knots into two thousand. One hundred hours. Four — say, five days — counting the flying. But — "

"But what?"

"What do we know about it? One of those things may be back tomorrow. Perhaps with the mail."

"By God! I hadn't thought of that!"

"Jack — get your banjo!"

It was an ecstatic evening, a long, hilarious night.

Then — day.

Henry went — almost without sleep — to the bay and sailed out a little distance in his boat. The storm had abated but heavy swells were moving in rows through the mouth of the harbor. He sat there on the water watching the sky.

With the coming of night he and the others were ready to admit that possibly no airship was being sent to them. Or else that they had overestimated speeds. Or that it took considerable time to prepare a ship. Or—

Rationalization made everything less obvious.

They built a fire on the bare rock at the headlands— a huge fire that made a star visible over many miles of water. They fired the heap of debris on top of Mount McCobb.

Jack tended the headland fire. Henry carried wood all night to the flames on the mountain.

Occasionally he lay down beside them and tried to sleep, but his ears were always attuned to catch the magical sound of a motor.

They ate very little.

On the second day the fires were still going, although they had relented the pace of feeding them. On the third, exhausted, they all slept. Not all at once— but by turns.

"Probably," Stone said, and his first assumption was very close to the truth, "they only fly out to sea once in a great while. Probably they're sending a boat. In a day or two— "

Keep the fires going. Make them into smudges by day. Huge columns of smoke— like the Lord leading the Children of Israel— stiff-standing above the summit of McCobb and swinging in the little wind over the water.

On the fourth day they were worn by the strain. They sat silent most of the time— attending to the fires regularly, climbing the mountain until all were foot-weary— hurrying to the beach with axes.

On the fifth day they remained beside the shore, straining their eyes.

The sixth was like it. The sun came out and it was warm. Beds in the house went unmade. Weeds gained in the gardens. No one shaved.

A week after the electrical day found them still in good
spirits. There were plenty of possibilities.

"Any day, now. Maybe they can't travel in airships or in boats
as fast as we'd thought."

"Any day. Of course. I believe that those fellows didn't know
within a long way of where they were. Too cloudy to navigate
and probably hard in a thing like that anyway. They've doubtless sent a ship and it may take a long time for that ship to
locate us. Maybe even a month."

Henry swallowed his impatience. "A month?"

"Why not? It's a big ocean and the island's a small speck.
Keep the fires going."

"Maybe — "

Someone frowned at Henry. Maybe the ocean was too
big and the island too small. Maybe the airship had never
reached — land.

Stone sat on the porch, his cane between his knees. Henry lay
on his back at his father's feet. Both men seemed weary. There
were circles under their eyes and their skins were haggard and
drawn over their cheek bones.

Down on the headland a fire — a small fire in comparison
to those that once had raged there — sent a single desultory
plume of smoke into the vacant air.

It was a month, that day, since the visitor from the skies
had fled overhead.

"It couldn't happen to us twice," Henry said in a strangled
voice.

His father did not answer.

McCobb appeared at the door and murmured that it looked
like rain. As if in answer, a string snapped on Jack's banjo,
which had been lying mute in the living room for thirty days.

Stone never rebounded from the catastrophe. He lost all interest in the schemes that the others invented to explain the
silence. Once, when Henry suggested that the men in the air

vessel had possibly believed the islanders were there as free men and had merely reported the existence of the island, and that someone sooner or later would come to verify the report, Stone had said, "Bosh."

It was his last spark. A negative spark. An admission of surrender.

He had borne for a great many years a full knowledge of the awfulness of his misdeed. He had paid a hundred times over for its rashness.

Stone had been a mighty man. New York had called him brilliant and aggressive. Paris had called him Spartan. In London he was evaluated as shrewd and acquisitive.

He had planned to perfection one of the most audacious human experiments ever made — to perfection if it may be overlooked that he neglected to supply a way for the return of his adventurers.

In the early years of the colonization of Stone Island it had been his brain and his spirit that furnished the driving force. He had led three men from despair to actual joy. He had founded and energized a new world.

But now his strength was taken away. Remorse and disappointment had shorn him. The eagle was fallen.

Day after day he sat beside the window in his chair, an old man, a Napoleon on Elba, planning escapes he was impotent to perform, hoping for miracles, and knowing that his doom was to be both certain and slow.

If one ship flew over, another will.

He did not even react to that.

They tried everything to bring him from himself. Their attempts were pitiful — because in them was the humiliation and misery of their own souls.

McCobb made a special omelet. Eat, a little, Viking. Eat. You've sat there with no food and only your wine for days.

Days.

Henry brought a necklace from the ruins.

Look, father, it's beautiful. A word carved on every stone. Handiwork unparalleled in Egypt or even Greece.

Silence.

They tried mock anger

Get yourself out of it. This is no behavior for a man.

Words used to children — and he was a child, sitting there and staring at emptiness.

By and by he got up. He shaved. He made his bed. He changed his clothes. He dined with them. He went out in the sun and weeded in the garden.

But he never smiled again.

He seldom spoke.

One day his hair turned snow-white. A pompom of white hair above the crag of his brow.

His steps faltered.

"What shall we do?" Henry asked anxiously of McCobb.

"What can we do, son? His fire has burned out. Like the fires down on the point. With them."

"But — "

"I know. I know."

"We're no worse off than we were before," Henry insisted. "And that makes twice. The third time — they'll take us back."

"The third time," McCobb repeated huskily and Henry, looking at him, realized that he, also, was old.

They found Stone on the 6th of June.

He was lying beside his wheelbarrow. He had been carrying manure from the goat corral to the garden.

He looked as if he had fallen asleep.

McCobb, who had come upon him first, summoned Jack.

"He's dead, Jack."

"Yes, Mr. McCobb."

"Where's Henry?"

"On the bay."

"Ring the bell."

"Yes, Mr. McCobb."

The Scotchman met Henry on the porch. "Your father died

this afternoon. A heart attack. It must have been instanta-
neous, and there's no sign of any pain."

Henry walked inside the house and sat down beneath the
sections of newspaper, which had been framed behind glass
that once had formed the bridge windows of the *Falcon*.

"We all expected it, didn't we?" he said slowly.

"We did, Henry. He's been failing for a long time."

"He was— fairly old."

"Almost seventy."

"Where is he?"

"I— I haven't moved him yet. He fell under that tree with
purple flowers."

"Oh."

They went out together— McCobb with his arm encircling
Henry's broad back.

They buried Stephen Stone inside the compound at the
foot of the huge tree on which he had first laid his hand— the
only tree of any size within the confines of the stockade. His
headstone was a boulder and on the face of it McCobb fixed a
plate of solid gold:

STEPHEN STONE

The days were long, after that. The house seemed strangely
empty. That emptiness frightened them.

It was in their eyes when they looked at each other.

Next.

It was in Henry's soul when he went to the edge of the sea
and whispered to the water: "I'll be last. I'll be there alone.
Alone with three graves. And I shall go mad."

McCobb came after him that day, as he had done once
before.

They sat together.

"Any day, now— "

"I'm thirty-one," Henry answered tonelessly. "And I have
been waiting all these years for any day."

"The cities"— McCobb murmured his list— "and women."

"Women!"

"Women— laddie— "

Henry rose. "Why torture me with it? I shall be last. I'll fish here alone. You will lie there and Jack. And I shall laugh and run on the beach and scream like a parrot. I'll never see a woman. I'll never— never— never— "

"Henry!"

"Oh— right. I'm sorry."

His resignation was worse than his anger. And in his heart McCobb admitted that all he said was true, all he felt was justified.

McCobb watched through the glasses. He knew what was going to happen — it had happened before.

Henry, stark naked, poised on the gunwale of the boat and dove.

His body flashed in the sun and McCobb could see the long knife in his hand.

Jack came out on the porch. He followed the direction of McCobb's glasses.

"What's he doing?"

"Watch."

The ripples that Henry's dive had started ran toward the shore. There was a very brief interval of calm. Then the whole surface of the bay in the neighborhood of the boat was broken by a mighty threshing.

In the foamy melee Henry came to the surface and swam quickly to the boat. He caught the gunwale and climbed aboard. He stuck the knife in the wood of a seat.

"Gor!" Jack murmured. "What is it?"

"Shark." McCobb bit off the word.

The splashing was already lessening. Red flowed in the froth. The motion of a long tail was visible, and the fish twisted round and round.

Henry saw McCobb on the porch and waved to him.

"He dive in and kill a big shark like that?" Jack asked.

"He did."

"With a knife?"

"With a knife. One just like that weapon you carry around."

"Damn!"

McCobb said nothing. The shark's motions were feeble now, and Henry was paddling toward it.

"That's dangerous," Jack said tentatively.

"You bet it is."

"What's he do it for?"

"Fun."

"For fun?"

"Yes, Jack."

"That ain't fun."

"For him it is. He's sick of things — just like you and me, Jack. Only he's young. We can swallow our feelings and say nothing. He can't. He has to go out and do things. The more dangerous the better."

"Sure enough?"

"That's the way boys like that are made." Suddenly McCobb turned and smiled at Jack in a manner almost brotherly. He could smile — now that the shark was lying with its ripped belly toward the sky. "You ought to know. I remember once Mr. Stone mentioned that you used to raise cane when you were a young buck."

Jack grinned and scratched his woolly head. "That's a fact." Doubt came in his face. "But I wouldn't of done nuthing like that. Not me."

McCobb laughed.

Henry made fast his shark and rowed laboriously toward the beach. Even through the glasses McCobb could see the flexing of his muscles.

Half an hour later the shark-killer appeared, bringing a portion of the hide.

"You saw my day's catch?"

McCobb nodded.

"I took this for shoosies and threw the rest back."

"It never occurred to you that you might get hurt doing that, did it, Henry?"

"Oh — no. Never."

"Never thought that three or four of those things might come at you simultaneously?"

Henry stopped and considered with mock seriousness. "Now that you mention it, Mr. McCobb — "

"Wouldn't mean anything to you if I asked you to take it easy — for Jack's and my sake?"

Henry shook his head up and down rapidly. "Sure. I'll stop."

"And you might abandon the idea that you can get one of the crocodiles barehanded, too."

"It's abandoned."

McCobb was embarrassed. "I'm not trying to supplant the place of your father. But — you see — if anything happened to you I'd feel responsible for cheating you out of your life — up there." He pointed toward the north.

"It's all right. I was just looking for a little excitement. There isn't much here anymore."

"I know."

Both men stared over the porch rail. Two traveler's trees spread fans like peacocks' tails in the yard. Beyond them, ebonies and eucalyptus and a member of the banyan family whose numerous gray trunks ran to earth like the probosces of elephants. Over all a redundancy of foliage with caves in it where the sun shot down, and birds whose plumage made them look like small fragments of a rainbow.

After that came the sea, so blue that the eyes ached in contemplation of it, and the shoals where the water turned to jade green and tan and even, along the coral edges, a pure alabaster white.

A scene indescribably beautiful and to them unutterably tedious. They had grown careless of the garden, and flowers bloomed there in a rank luxury of competition, overwhelming each other and threatening to inundate the house itself.

Days passed again.

Henry settled into an inactivity that to McCobb was worse than his foolhardy pursuit of stimulating dangers. He did not read, he did not work, he ate and slept and was silent.

Months.

They seldom rallied each other. The flow of life was slowing down and because Henry had ceased to care, the others had somehow lost interest.

When the ship came, they did not see it at all. Jack was making preparations for lunch. McCobb was in his shop. Henry sat with a book on his knees and his eyes closed.

He heard sounds come over the water of the bay. Oarlocks creaked and there were voices. His stultified subconscious suggested that McCobb had gone fishing.

Then he realized that the voices were not those of his own companions.

With legs like water, he went to the porch.

A lifeboat, rowed by a half dozen sailors, was already halfway into the bay. A man stood in the stern with the tiller in his hands. It was his voice that Henry had heard — for he was stroking his sailors.

Henry opened his mouth and shouted for McCobb with every ounce of his power — and not a sound issued from his throat. Sweat broke out upon him. His tongue clove to the roof of his mouth. Once again he tried, and a sort of scream was the result.

McCobb at that moment came around the house, and trees prevented him from seeing the bay.

"What ails you, lad? Are you choking?"

Henry's ashen face swung toward the water and McCobb hurried to his side. He remembered later that he thought Henry was seeing a great beast emerging from the ocean. He did not think of men.

Next, he was hugging Henry. "There it is, lad," he whispered. "There's home. There they come. See how finely they row? Straight for the sand. Seven of them, Henry! Now — are you having a thrill?"

Henry didn't speak.

"We've got to go down and meet them," McCobb gibbered. His glee was ghastly. "That's the proper function of a host."

He started to pull Henry toward the steps. But Henry turned. He pointed toward the kitchen.

"That's right." McCobb had a spasm of shaking and his breath hissed between his teeth. "Jack."

The word was inaudible. "Call him, son."

"Jack!" Suddenly Henry's voice was let loose and it echoed across the bay so vehemently that the sailors stopped rowing and turned to look at the shore.

"Yes, Mr. Henry?" The Negro's words came peacefully through the house. He stood beside them.

"Dreams," he said mysteriously. "Dreams."

"Come!" McCobb tottered across the compound.

They reached the sand just as the small boat grounded and the sailors jumped into the shallow water. The run down the road had restored them somewhat.

McCobb went first. He held out his hand to the gaping officer.

"My name's McCobb. David McCobb. This is Mr. Stone and our man Jack. We're glad to see you — " He got no further. He was seized by a paroxysm of weeping.

The officer and his men stared. They stared at the clothes, at the faces, and at the house. One or two of them whispered in a language that the islanders could not understand.

Henry mastered his wonderment. "We — we don't know what to say. You see — we've been here for thirty-three years."

Then the officer spoke. He spoke rapidly and they did not understand a syllable. He turned to his men and lifted his hand. The men cheered and waved their hats.

McCobb had recovered again. "They're Scandinavians, Henry. They probably don't know a word of English. But it doesn't matter." He beckoned toward them and turned to Jack. "Come on, Jack. We'll take them to the house and get dinner for them. A big dinner."

The officer — a short, blond man — came to life. He stepped forward and embraced the islanders. He pounded their backs. And the men mingled with them. There was, abruptly, an immense confusion — a confusion that was partly allayed as McCobb began to pull and beckon them toward the house. They went up the road.

As they walked, the officer came beside Henry. He seemed

to be asking a question. He repeated it — pointing to the sea and holding up first two fingers and then five and finally ten. Henry was so breathless from this contact with the fourth person he had seen in his life that it was some time before he understood.

Then, nodding, smiling, talking nonsense, he held up all ten fingers three times and three fingers more.

The officer shook his head and shouted to his men that the castaways had been on the island for thirty-three years. Astonishment swept over them.

Then they went through the corral gate. McCobb swept his arm across the compound. "Our home, gentlemen."

Jack was babbling to one of the sailors, who regarded him with a fantastic concentration and nodded every time he spoke. McCobb and Henry took the arms of the officer, as if they feared he would get away.

The new arrivals on Stone Island went over the home and possessions of the trio they had discovered with shouts of amazement. Everything astounded them — the building itself, the goats and chickens, the kitchen, the gold ornaments, the arms in the living-room closet. They gathered in groups and declaimed to each other on every new discovery.

McCobb at last brought a bottle of whisky.

The mate lifted his drink. "Skoal!"

McCobb answered, "Skoal!"

Everyone roared with laughter. Seldom on earth has such excitement existed in the hearts of men.

Laughter, tears, handshaking, oration, shouts, whispers — for half an hour everything was madness.

Then the mate made a short speech and pointed toward the sea. They returned to the porch. Over the tops of the trees on the headland, two masts were visible.

They went back to the shore. But when the sailors pushed off, Henry, McCobb, and Jack scrambled into their boat and followed with imploring cries.

The act was so pitiful that it made the trip to the ship rela-
tively silent.

"Look, laddie."

Henry stopped rowing for a moment and followed McCobb's
finger. The ship was small. A freighter. She was low in the water
and her sides were rusted. The deck was lined with men and
on the bridge the captain leaned out and stared at the second
boat with profound astonishment.

The scene on deck was a repetition of the scene on shore,
save that the mate who had commanded the small boat went
immediately into a tirade of explanation.

Then the captain took their hands and spoke a number of
words that were obviously intended as a welcome. After that
McCobb tried to clarify things. Henry intervened with French,
which was received with smiles and shakes of the head, and
then with German — which the captain understood slightly.

That understanding was all that was needed.

Glasses clinked in the captain's cabin and he stumblingly
expressed his wish to see the island home for himself. They
arranged, then, to dine there. Jack went ahead with the ship's
cook. The others followed.

The afternoon was a fury of industry. Henry and the captain
and one of the mates climbed Mount McCobb. The men from
the sea stared spellbound at the land.

McCobb packed. The sailors cleared out all the vegetables
from the garden and transferred them to the *Cjoda*. They took
the chickens and the goats and ten of the zebus. The rest of
the zebus were turned loose.

The abundance of gold in the house astonished the sailors
and two or three of them made away with some of McCobb's
ornaments. The gems they did not see, and the Scotchman
secreted some on his person and the rest in the trunks. The
Scotchman also opened one of the last of the copper drums.
It contained clothes. He transferred them to a trunk. Also he
took many papers and notebooks and maps.

Later in the afternoon the men returned from the mountain. Jack had dinner ready at six. The sailors were fed on the porch and the officers sat with Henry and McCobb in the living room. Roast meat, baked potatoes, beets, carrots, fruit, and wine.

The sailors were sent back with one officer to the ship that night, but the captain and the mate who had first reached shore stayed in the house. By signs, in halting German, and with much excitement, the islanders told the story of their arrival and their long sojourn.

Henry could not think consecutively for more than a few seconds. "Aren't the men fine looking?" he said to McCobb, and the Scot, who had seen better men, agreed. "They're going round Good Hope to New York. They'll take us straight — home." McCobb nodded and twisted the stem of his glass in his fingers. "Was denken sie — " "Ja. Drei und dreissig Jahren. Mein vater — "

Through the night to dawn. The captain slept. But Henry did not sleep and McCobb did not sleep and Jack's slumbers were punctuated by strange writhings, and once by laughter.

Henry stood with McCobb on the stern deck of the *Cjoda*. Her engines clanked and foamy water poured away from her rusted hull. Stone Island moved backward. Soon they were as far from it as Henry had ever sailed. The trees melted into one green coast. The mountain became sharply delineated against the blue sky. Its edges lost their precision. The green began to grow blue.

"My heart hurts," Henry said slowly.

"Yes, son."

"I can't keep my eyes off the men. It's impossible to believe that there are so many of them."

"I know."

"They all look exactly alike."

"You'll get over that."

"I think I could spend a year on this ship without ever minding it."

"You'll get over that, too."

"We're not going to make any other port. It'll be about seven weeks. Think! Only seven weeks! I wish the captain and I could understand each other better."

"Look at the island, lad. You may never see it again."

"I'll come back."

"I'm wondering."

A long silence.

"Happy, McCobb?"

"I'm the happiest old man on earth."

"You're not old."

McCobb laughed. "I've even got no right to be active at my age. But the life was healthy. I feel like a young fellow of fifty-five."

"I feel old."

"Humph. The reason they didn't believe we'd been here so long is because you look so young — in spite of the mustache. I had to show 'em our records. Even then — they didn't quite think it was true. Not until they saw the sills were rotting under the house and until they saw the apple trees. After that — they did believe me."

"I wonder what it will be like?"

"I don't know."

In the tiny wireless room of the *Cjoda* the operator was flashing the news of the finding of three Americans on a hitherto unknown island. But the news did not travel far. It was printed in a South African paper. The Associated Press missed it. The tramp freighter would steam unhailed for many weeks.

McCobb sighed. "If your father could have lived — "

"I've thought of that many times — since yesterday."

"The island's almost gone now."

"Yes."

From amidships came the sound of Jack's banjo and an accompaniment of laughter.

McCobb located Henry. Henry hung over the rail of the bridge and watched the men work. He never tired of watching them.

His interest was like that of an entomologist who has found a new species.

McCobb was excited. "Henry! There's an instrument on this ship that sends messages through the air!"

"No! Where to?"

"God knows where. Everywhere. They can send a message ashore."

"Good Lord!"

"Those wires up there are part of it. The fellow who sits in that little house yonder does it with a key like a telegraph key."

They stared in stunned silence.

"We can let them know in New York— "

Henry nodded. "Sure. If such a thing is possible. A few days before we get in— no use bothering anybody now. Nobody to bother anyway— except my father's lawyers— or their firm."

"That's right. Then— maybe— they'll send someone to meet us. We may need somebody. There will probably be a lot of newfangled things we won't understand. Like this thing that telegraphs through the air. Come on and look at it."

The grinning operator allowed them to listen to a flow of dots and dashes through his headphones. They modestly planned to announce their rescue and arrival when they were a few days off shore. They hoped that someone would meet them. They had a poor notion of the drama their arrival would cause.

Old Elihu Whitney — he was over eighty — sat in the library of his penthouse. The full beard that had replaced his mutton-chop whiskers was now white. His body had shrunk, so that his clothes hung a little loosely upon him, but he would not send new measurements to his tailor. His face was patrician and as bold as it had always been. He was somewhat restive — he had been incessantly restive since his formal retirement from business — but the only signs of it were the impatience and fidgetiness with which he unfolded his newspaper and spread a napkin on his lap.

It was his custom to breakfast in the library, sitting in front of the French windows that overlooked first a balcony and then a panorama of the summits of Manhattan.

The windows were open — for it was early June.

While he fiddled with his food and scanned the paper through his spectacles his granddaughter momentarily appeared at the door.

"Going out," she said.

He turned and smiled. His reward was a flash — a glitter — bright eyes, bright hair, bright smile, bright clothes.

"Did you get up this early or have you been up?"

She laughed in the hall.

He heard the elevator hum and the shunt and slam of the door. He sighed. There was a reference to him in the paper. "Dean of the New York bar," it said. Elihu Whitney grunted with a disapproval that was not real.

The telephone rang.

He beat his butler to it by a yard and scowled at the man ferociously.

"Elihu Whitney speaking!" His voice still had the power to boom.

"Yes," he said. He passed his hand over his beard. "Eh? Radio message? Castaways? What's that?" A new note came in his voice. "Listen, Sid. Be sure that's the name. Be certain it was Henry Stone, son of Stephen. Because if it is— "

He hung up.

He stood in the center of the room and swore. He swore like a soldier, with glee and gusto and variety. His old hands were doubled into gnarled fists. His eyes were full of fire. "What a thing! What a thing! Thank God I lived. It can't be! It would be! I wonder— no. Yes. It would happen that way. Stephen would— "

"Beg pardon, sir?"

"Oh— Stokes— get the hell out of here."

"Yes, sir."

"No— don't. Don't go. Wait. Good God, what a blow this will be to the directorate. What a shock to Voorhees. I wonder if he'll be competent? If Stephen trained him? Maybe— "

"You feel all right, sir?"

Whitney stiffened and realized that his incoherence must have sounded strange. "I never felt better in my life, Stokes. Never. I feel like a spring lamb. And I'm going to do a little bit of work, Stokes. I think I am. I wouldn't be surprised if it was my masterpiece."

"Yes, sir."

Whitney paced the floor. "Get Sid back on the wire."

He took the instrument. "Sid? Your father. You're sure?"

"We radioed for confirmation. The ship's a tramp. Out of Batavia coming to New York. First trip here. Swenson Line docks. Captain vouched for everything and the Swenson people say he's thoroughly reliable. The message was from the men. Just a formal notification and a request to be met. The signature was David McCobb— name of the engineer he took in Liverpool in eighteen-ninety-seven— and Henry Stone."

"It's unbelievable."

"We're pretty excited down here, of course. That's why I

called you. It means that all the Stone properties will be turned over— a big order. Twenty-two newspapers, now, you know. And Voorhees's gang will be subject to him. Raise hell with politics. That is— unless he's non compos— "

"I know what it will do. Keep it quiet, will you?"

"Can't. The Swenson Line got the message first. They let it out."

"What?"

"They turned it over to the papers. Good publicity for them, I suppose. We've had fifty calls an hour ever since. The whole *Record* staff is parked in our office now. Voorhees called up and he was wild."

"What did he say?"

"He said he was running the show in this town and he intended to keep on running it, new owner or no new owner. Then he sputtered for a while. Then he said he'd fight any effort to interfere with him from here to hell."

"What did you say?"

"I said that nobody had made any effort to interfere with him."

"Yes?"

"That's all. He knows you and I can't touch him while he keeps the bankbooks in order and the profits high. He knows this Stone— if he comes— can reorganize all twenty-two papers in two hours if he wants to. So I told him that Stone was a naked savage who couldn't speak a word of English."

"Is he?" Whitney asked, his heart in his mouth.

"The actual description is pretty terse and I've managed to keep that much dark. But I gather from it that he's anything but a naked savage."

Whitney's heart beat again. "He's Stephen Stone's son, Sid. Stephen's and Nellie Larsen's. And God makes people like them once in a long time. I tell you— hell is loose."

The lawyer hung up and sat down in his chair. He laughed like a boy. He slapped his thigh. Tears streamed down his face.

"If he's only like his father! If he's only like Stephen," Whitney repeated. "There'll be hell to pay and blood in the street and Voorhees— oh, boy!— Voorhees will have to move to Timbuktu and raise pigeons!"

Henry wore a Prince Albert. His black tie was neatly knotted on his white shirt. Cloth-topped shoes hurt his feet. The top hat on his head was a size too small and he had to hold it in place with his hand.

He stood at the rail and stared at the lights of the distant city. They rose like a fountain of fire to breathless heights. The *Cjoda* rode at anchor in the bay.

McCobb tugged at the coat. "Laddie! I've been speaking to you."

"I'm sorry."

"Look at it."

"I'm looking."

"They've built it higher than the mountains. Did you ever dream of such buildings? I can't believe my eyes. But I can catch a glimpse of the old Battery there— and that's familiar. It makes me ache to see it. The rest is crazy."

"It's— it's— "

"I know. Did ye see the ship on the other side?"

"I did."

It was the *Leviathan*, riding at Quarantine. They could not say any more, but stood with locked arms, staring dazedly at the mountain of light that was Manhattan.

A launch came alongside. Men climbed aboard. They were directed aft by the captain. McCobb and Henry turned from their rapture.

One of the men stepped forward. "Mr. McCobb? Mr. Stone? I'm Sidney Whitney."

The sound of familiar English startled both men. Henry stretched out his hand in the dark.

"Thank you for coming."

"You're Stone, eh?" Henry could feel the scrutiny. "Well— I

congratulate you on your homecoming." The voice was warm and excitement ran through it.

"We cannot say much," Henry replied. "We are both — overcome." The long lessons in manners and conversation seemed to desert him. He felt half blind and his limbs were heavy.

"I can understand." Mr. Whitney took McCobb's hand. "My father — Elihu Whitney — is waiting off shore. I've arranged to take you off in a launch."

"Yes."

Dully, they followed Whitney. They went over the side of the ship — McCobb with greater ease than the lawyer's son. They sat in the launch. It rushed over the obsidian river toward the pile of stars that made the skyscrapers.

"We forgot Jack!" Henry said.

Mr. Whitney leaned toward him. "We arranged for his disembarkation in the morning. All this is irregular. It required considerable — maneuvering."

"Oh."

"Couldn't I go back and stay with him?" McCobb asked suddenly. His tone revealed that he had been crying.

"If you like."

"I'd rather. I'd prefer to come into all this in daylight — slowly," McCobb said.

The launch put back. Then it left the *Cjoda* again, making a great half-circle of foam. Whistles boomed. Tugs and ferries slid over the water. The small boat rocked on their swells. Nobody spoke to Henry — and he was glad. He never took his eyes from the skyscrapers.

In the seat beside him, Whitney regarded him with as much attention as he gave the buildings. What the lawyer saw satisfied him.

The boat reached a pier and dove into the shadows. Its motor died. It bumped. Henry stepped upon the shores of America.

The pier was covered and its vast, crate-filled interior was only dimly lighted. Sidney Whitney hurried him through it. At the far end was a door. Beyond the door, the street. And standing in the street was a vehicle. No horses were attached to it. A door in its side opened. Whitney propelled him through it.

Henry found himself in a little room that was lighted. A large, old man sat in it on a long seat.

"Dad, this is Henry Stone."

"Sit here." They shook hands. Henry sat. The little room — the entire vehicle — moved forward. It gained speed rapidly and, although curtains were drawn over the windows, Henry knew that the speed was considerable.

He looked at the other men. They had stretched out their feet so he stretched out his feet. They were looking at him — Sidney Whitney even leaning around his father — and they did not seem to be interested in the jolting and swinging of the vehicle, so he tried to ignore it. Once, however, on a turn, he lost his balance and grasped with an involuntary wildness for support.

"There's a little cord," Elihu Whitney said in a kind voice.

"Oh. Thanks. I'm afraid I'm a trifle awkward. I haven't ridden in anything like this, you see — "

"Good Lord! That's right. My God, Stone, I apologize. I should have warned you about the turns."

Henry smiled. "No harm done. What's it called?"

"It's a Rolls-Royce. That is to say — it's an automobile."

"From the Latin, eh?"

Whitney senior sucked in his breath and stared at the young man. "Yes. Do you know Latin?"

"Just a bit," Henry answered. "Livy and Pliny."

"Your father — you don't mind if I am rather brutally frank and curious — your father educated you?"

Henry nodded. "We had a large library, of course. We tried to make my education, in so far as it was formalized, a copy of the usual college course for the degrees of Bachelor of Arts and Bachelor of Science. Then father had me study for a PhD and an MA, which he eventually awarded. I'm afraid" — Henry's smile was pleasant — "my degrees wouldn't have much standing and my knowledge is certainly antiquated, but it was the best we could do."

"When— when did Stephen— ?"

"In nineteen-twenty-nine," Henry replied. "Of heart failure. We found him in the garden."

"I see. He was a great man, your father."

"He was."

"I suppose he told you all about himself?"

Henry nodded. "There was plenty of time to talk."

"Yes." Elihu Whitney peered through the curtains. "We stole you off the ship— for various reasons. I imagine you know that you will immediately fall heir to your father's papers?"

"Yes. He did everything in his power to make me thoroughly equipped to run them."

"Then he thought you'd come back?"

"He hoped."

"Oh. I presume that you realize your father's properties have expanded? They now embrace twenty-two newspapers in all the large cities, and eleven banks."

Henry started. "No!"

"Valued at something like two hundred and eighty million dollars and perhaps the most influential section of the country's press under one head. The head— of course— is the self-perpetuating committee left by your father."

Henry looked dazedly at the lawyer. "I didn't guess that. Of course— I'll simply have to let the men in office continue. I am a babe in the woods."

Whitney did not answer because the car stopped. Henry had a glimpse of brilliant lobby, an interminable elevator ride that, by its revelation of flashing doors, gave him a better idea of the height of the buildings than his observations from the bay, and they were in the Whitney library.

The three men stood there— all of them silent with wonder.

Whitney inadvertently offered a cigar to Henry and was surprised when he took it. He was on the point of warning the young man when Henry spoke for himself. "This is certainly fine tobacco. We had our own plants on the island— but none of our cigars could be compared with this one."

Sidney Whitney did not stay. He made his apologies and departed— after one lingering look at the islander.

Elihu waved Henry into a chair. "Now. It will be hard to know where to begin and what to say. First— I'm going to insist that you accept my hospitality for the time being. I'm afraid— "

"That's immensely kind of you."

"Good. One thing settled. Now— I can't give you a history of the world since eighteen-ninety-seven in a few minutes, but I'll tell you what I think of. And I'll tell you about your papers. They're run by a man named Voorhees, who, to my way of thinking, is corrupt. But I can't remove him as long as his policy is financially successful— and that it has certainly been. He's a politician, and a liar. A thief and a grafter. I'm telling that to you as your lawyer.

"I'll go into the details of New York corruption with you later. But I imagine"— and it was only Whitney's keenness of imagination that started him off on so accurate a track— "that you'll want to know first about airplanes and the radio and these buildings. About science and medicine and the war. About the world. To begin with— "

Whitney talked. He talked for two hours— refreshing himself sometimes from his vivid memory of the world in 1897 and sometimes from the face of the man who sat before him. Henry drank his words. Every syllable stuck in his mind.

It was after the second hour of that amazing recital that Marian Whitney came into the room. She came in quickly from the elevator— still wearing a hat and a fur. She had a newspaper under her arm. She scarcely noticed Henry— her eyes, in fact, did not even reach his face. She was bursting with excitement. She must have concluded subconsciously that he was some business visitor from the hinterland.

"Grandfather! Grandfather! The most priceless thing has

happened! Probably you knew it and didn't tell me." Whitney tried to halt her, but there was no chance. "They've found Stephen Stone's son. They've brought him from a desert island. He's a savage. He can't say a word in any language and he has big toes. He goes naked and snaps at people. He's as hairy as a monkey. Here's a special issue of the *Record* — telling all about it, and suggesting that he be put in the zoo since he obviously can't do anything."

She thrust the paper into her grandfather's hands and looked up at him. He had just winked very slowly at Henry.

But Henry had not seen the wink.

His face was bloodless.

The great muscles on his jaws were knotty.

His hands hung limp

He stared at Marian. At her piquant black hat. At the golden hair that showed beneath it. At her white brow and her arched eyebrows, her great blue eyes, her scarlet lips, the curve of her throat and the curve of her breast, the shape of her body, the silken stockings that covered her legs invisibly and the shoes on her feet. And he had heard her voice. No one had ever told him about a woman's voice!

She turned toward him. Their eyes met. Marian stepped back, but she could not tear away her gaze. She had never seen anything like it.

He was a volcano.

His shoulders were hunched, as if he were lifting the world.

His eyes went black and liquid.

His hands clenched.

He began to tremble.

Elihu Whitney, at first, thought that he had been taken violently ill. Then he understood and a compassion dreadful in its intensity mastered him.

A clock ticked.

The corners of Henry's mouth twitched — as if he were trying to smile — but the imitation was ghastly.

Marian, after eternity, said, "I'm sorry."

The words relaxed everyone — made them remember that they were people.

Henry suddenly bowed and said, "I beg your pardon."

Whitney found some sort of voice. "The newspaper lied grossly, Marian. This is — the savage. My granddaughter, Mr. Stone."

She stepped toward him and he watched her approach like a man watching the flight of an angel. Her hand was under his eyes.

"I'm awfully sorry. I didn't mean to be — cruel."

He took her hand.

The room was still.

"I have been rude," Henry said. Each word was pronounced with a gigantic effort. "You see — I've never seen a woman before."

"Oh!" It was a small outcry. She glanced frantically at her grandfather.

He nodded gravely. He appreciated that he was the witness of a drama that, perhaps, had never before occurred on earth.

"Never seen a woman?" she repeated.

He bent forward, as if to catch every faint inflection of her voice.

"I lived — all my life — on an island — where there were — no women."

"I see."

"Why don't we sit down?" Whitney said.

They sat. He stared at her and suddenly she seemed to be glad that he was staring at her, to be unashamed and unembarrassed at the darkened eyes that made a conquest of her detail by detail.

Finally he looked away.

They watched him. He was breathing slowly and deeply. He rubbed the arm of his chair with the palm of his hand. His eyes came back to her — a thirsty man who drinks and halts a moment only to drink again.

At last, from the dim resources of his mind, the breeding that his father had instilled in him reasserted itself. He smiled.

"How does it seem — to see a woman for the first time?" She asked the question seriously, impersonally.

Henry's eyes were calmer. "The sensation — is indescribable. But I believe I have been unduly fortunate — in that you are the first woman I have seen."

Marian looked at her grandfather. "They said he was a savage."

Whitney chuckled. The crisis had passed.

"That was Sid's idea — he told it to Voorhees. And Voorhees made the most of it. He wouldn't want anyone to know that Stephen's son was — "

Marian glanced at the man with the mustache, the man with the Prince Albert. "Exactly," she said. Then she turned to Henry. "Talk to me."

"I'd rather listen to you."

"That's pretty — and it may even be true. But you've got to talk. Tell me about the time — oh — anything. Tell me about the island. What was it like? What did you eat? What did you wear? How did you amuse yourself?"

In her eyes he saw interest and something that was like adulation. His father's warnings flickered through his mind. Was not this — this attraction — the first step toward destruction?

Whitney intervened. "Go ahead, Henry. Tell us." He wanted the young man to talk. He wanted to listen to his voice and accent and judge his vocabulary and measure his mind.

Henry began painfully. "It really wasn't anything, I should think, that would interest you. The island was about twenty miles long — from east to west — and fifteen miles wide at the widest part. The geology of it — "

No one interrupted him. No one looked at the time. Whitney had talked for two hours about modern civilization. Henry talked for three about the island. The fascination of his audience tricked him into forgetting himself.

"And I looked"— Henry found himself saying— "and it was a lifeboat full of men."

The silence was better than any applause.

Whitney took his watch from his vest pocket.

"Four?" Marian guessed.

"That's right. I'll take you to your rooms— mind if I call you Henry?"

"I'd be delighted— "

Marian stood and stretched. "Good night— Henry."

"Good night, Miss Whitney."

"You don't mind if I fall in love with you, do you?"

"Ah— " She was gone. Henry looked blankly at her grandfather.

"That's Marian's way of having fun."

"Oh."

Henry was so weary, when he shut the door of his elaborate suite, that he had almost no strength to glean new impressions. He entered the bathroom, however, looked at its tile and metal, and laughed. When he put on the pajamas that had been laid out for him and thrust himself between the sheets, he exclaimed aloud. He had not dreamed of such a bed.

He shut his eyes. For a few frantic moments his brain revolved. He was sure that he would spend a night as sleepless as his last night at sea. But in a few moments he was deep in slumber.

He opened his eyes and stared with bewilderment at the ceiling. Memory of the last twenty-four hours rushed over him. He took his watch from beneath his pillow— a huge gold watch that had belonged to his father. Eleven-fifteen. He sat up. From his bed he could look through wide windows over the summits of New York. They glittered in the sun and he walked toward the wind-stirred curtains as if he were hypnotized.

He saw the city, heard it and smelled it. A fairyland of shining chrome steel— lofty, fantastic, incredibly beautiful— palisades and terraces and mighty shafts that lost themselves in the haze. A dim and yet pervasive roar from which separate sounds occasionally emerged— the trumpeting of an automobile horn, the chatter of a rivet hammer, the basso of a river whistle. A scent of smoke and steam and gasoline fumes— vague, acrid, stimulating.

He looked down at traffic, watching it stop and start, more in the manner of a colossal machine than of individual vehicles with private destinations.

Someone knocked on his door.

"Come."

A man entered. He carried a large tray through the bedroom and into the living room, which Henry had not investigated on the previous night.

"Your breakfast, sir."

"Thanks."

"Mr. Whitney has been shopping for you, sir. I believe that he has purchased a brown suit and a gray one. Which shall I lay out?"

Henry blushed. "It doesn't matter."

"Very well, sir. I shall return with the brown suit in half an hour. Shall I draw a bath?"

Henry was afraid that he would not be able to manage a bath in the complicated tile room. He shook his head in embarrassment. "No, thanks. I— no— thanks."

"Very well, sir."

Henry went into the living room. On the tray was an electric toaster and some bread. A patent egg-boiler that worked by electricity and used only a spoonful of water. A coffee machine made of two glass flasks. A grapefruit.

He stared at these things. The fruit he had never seen. The little machines he could not operate. He saw ice under the grapefruit— a nest of ice— and while he realized what it was after a moment's thought he did not know whether it was to be eaten or not. He took a piece in his fingers, learned its slipperiness and the burning sensation caused by its temperature.

Another knock at his door.

"Come in."

It was Marian in blue pajamas. Henry blushed again— not because of her costume but because he remembered her last words of the previous night. He did not mind the unconventionality of their clothes because he was accustomed to few clothes and because he did not know the conventions of this decade.

"Good morning."

"Good morning, Miss Whitney."

"I came to have breakfast with you. My tray is on the way."

He bowed from the waist. "That will be delightful."

"Do you always talk like that— and bow?"

"I— " His embarrassment increased.

Marian laughed. "Never mind. It's sweet. I just found out that grandfather played a joke on you. He ordered all the trick gadgets in the house on your tray to see what you'd do."

"Trick gadgets?"

"Those things. The toaster and the coffeemaker and the egg boiler."

She sat down and a maid brought her tray. "How did you sleep?"

"Perfectly, thank you. And you?"

"Me? Well enough. Now. I'll show you what to do. That wire goes to the plug there. Here!" She rose and arranged things for him. "You turn the toast with that dingus."

"Oh. A dingus?"

"Slang, Henry. That handle. You see. Watch the coffee. When it comes up, you turn off the heat. Two times. Then you pour it."

"What is this?"

"That's a grapefruit. You eat it first."

"It's very kind of you to take the trouble to initiate me into these mysteries."

She smiled. "It's only a beginning, Henry. Everyone in the house is crazy to take you around. Father came in a half hour ago — he was up all night — and I had to use force to get him into bed. Grandfather is probably sneaking around in the hall right now, peering through keyholes and listening at cracks."

"Oh."

"You mustn't be annoyed. We're all pretty proud of our city and civilization — except the way things are run." Henry was digging into his grapefruit. Marian's eye fell on the radio and she had an inspiration. She turned it on surreptitiously. In a moment a voice boomed softly: "Are you listening?"

Henry jumped and turned around. "Yes, indeed," he said.

Marian stifled her mirth. Jud Jackson's California Clippers began to play "Lowdown."

Henry put his grapefruit on the table. He found the source of the sound and walked to the radio cabinet.

At last he looked at the girl.

"What is it?"

"Jazz."

"A jazz?"

"Oh. The music is called jazz. It's for dancing."

"Sounds that way. Did Edison invent it? Is it the talking machine? Father used to tell me about that."

"It's a radio."

"Like the one on the ship?"

"Yes. But it brings sounds of all sorts — music and speeches — from all over the world. Without wires."

"How wonderful!" Henry listened to the music for a while. "I think I like it — and I think I don't. It's — it makes you feel strange."

"You're precocious."

He did not answer. The toast began to burn.

When they finished their breakfast, she rose. "I've got to go and dress." She saw his color mount. "These — are pajamas — for house wear. Do you like them?"

"I — I — I think they are very — charming."

"The reporters are waiting for you downstairs. You'll have to see them, I guess."

"Oh."

"And— do me a favor— will you?"

"Anything."

"Shave off the mustache."

Henry had finished the adventure of dressing. The valet had initiated him in the business of modern clothes. He had shaved away his drooping mustache. When he went into the library he afforded the twenty-odd men assembled there a breath-taking moment. He was taller than any of them— twice as broad as some, tan as walnut stain, and he walked with ease and pride.

His voice was deep and assured and his eyes moved candidly from face to face. He even smiled a little.

"Gentlemen, I put myself at your disposal."

There was a murmur. They had expected a man in a skin loin-skirt with matted hair and bloodshot eyes— an animal exhibition of grunts and teeth-baring. Voorhees had assured the world of that.

"Are you— Henry Stone?"

"I am."

"Jeest! How come you can talk English? Been learning on the boat?"

Henry's lips twitched. He stood in their midst. "My father taught me English when I was two or three— as your fathers did. You see, gentlemen, the *Record*, in publishing the description of me that you took as gospel, was somewhat misinformed. I am a savage— I suppose— according to your contemporary tenets. But— "

The *Record* feature writer began to make notes: "Shock of hair. Tree-climbing toes hidden under disguise of modern clothes. Talks fairly well— stilted dialect."

A man at his side thought: "The scion of his father— old-worldish but cultured and brilliant— and one of the most magnificent physical specimens this jaded metropolis has entertained for decades."

The first fifteen minutes of Henry's audience were felicitous. Then came a change. Someone asked, "What are you going to do with your papers?"

"I haven't decided."

"What's your political affiliation?"

"I have made none as yet."

"What do you think of Capone?"

"I never heard of him."

"What's your stand on Prohibition?"

"Prohibition of what?" They laughed.

"What do you think ought to be done with Muscle Shoals?"

"I don't know."

"How do you expect to manage anything when you don't know the difference between income tax and Liberty Bonds?"

"He means— Mr. Stone— "

Henry flushed. "I understand what he means. I shall have to inform myself as rapidly as possible."

"What do you think of necking?"

"Of what?"

They explained. Henry was horrified. "I can't see how my opinion would interest you. Or how— even— you could print it without a libel suit— "

"What about— "

They began to probe into Henry's private life. They asked him questions on topics that he had discussed with no one. They wrote answers for them all. And Henry began to lose patience with them. Their vulgarity, their bad manners, their insistence on replies wore away his willingness to meet any new situation with an open mind. When they began to ask questions about his father's love life, Henry rebelled.

"That will be all, gentlemen."

"Is it true he never had kissed any woman except her? Is that so?"

Henry looked blackly at the questioner.

"Is it true she quit him because he beat her?"

Henry stalked from the room and slammed the door.

Elihu Whitney found him in his own living room, sprawled in a chair, his face in his hands.

"What's the trouble?"

"The reporters!" Henry said furiously. "It was unspeakable! Malicious. Vulgar. Good Lord — "

"Don't mind them, boy. You don't dare mind them. They'll print worse things than they said. But you can't worry about it."

"I'll stop them. They can't print what they said about father."

"They can and they will."

"But it wasn't true."

"That makes no difference."

Henry paced back and forth across his room. "If that's what the newspaper business is — I don't want to be in it. I wouldn't have anything to do with it. It's filthy."

"Easy — son. By the way — it's twelve-thirty. We're taking you out to lunch and then for a tour of the town."

"I don't want — " Henry controlled himself somewhat. "Very well. I regret my temper. But — "

Whitney pulled his beard and looked at the young man with grave attention. "Forget it. Forget it."

Henry met Marian on the staircase. He was astonished again by her change in costume. As yet he had had no opportunity — even in hasty glances through the windows of the Whitney mansion — to observe the dress of modern women. Marian wore blue. A blue dress with a flimsy and meaningless blue jacket over it, and a blue hat. He realized that he was staring at her only when she laughed.

"You like my ensemble?"

"I beg your pardon?"

The sound of her laughter stopped but its accompanying smile lingered. "Honestly, Henry, by begging people's pardon every thirty seconds, by bowing to them, and rushing around eagerly to keep doors open and traffic cleared ahead of them, you're going to make a nervous wreck out of yourself."

He stood aside to let her pass by but she merely came another step closer and stood with her eyes level to his. "In this rude travesty of civilization good manners have vanished entirely. You probably began to gather that from the reporters."

Henry flushed. "They were despicable."

Marian's eyebrows went up. "You could find a shorter and more accurate word. Lousy, for example."

His flush deepened, but although he was embarrassed he stood unmoved and repeated her expression: "Lousy." Into his mind flashed a quick portrait of the green island, the long-lasting sunshine and his father's interminable dissertations on English usage.

"Anyway, you're game. Now you be a good boy and say 'lousy' a hundred times a day. Then after that I'll teach you how to say a lot of other words. I'll begin with the easy ones— 'snooty,' 'swell,' 'punk,' 'racket,' 'high-hat,' and on into the upper register of current argot. What shall I teach you after that, Henry?"

He had gained a little confidence in himself and banished from his mind the notion that it was absurd and not quite polite to stand face to face on a staircase while conversing with a young lady. "I'm sure I don't know." His smile was quite genuine, his eyes steadily upon hers.

"There are so many things, Henry. You smoke and drink, which is doing pretty well for an old desert-island boy. I wonder if you gamble? Do you know how to gamble, Henry?"

His discomfort under this gentle teasing had temporarily subsided. "I know how to play poker. I know the principles of roulette— father explained it to me very carefully. And five hundred."

"My! Henry, you're a rake-hell. Also you're a prevaricator. The picture of quiet life on the island that you gave last night is fading fast. I had imagined your days were like one long

Sunday afternoon. But what do I find? Poker! Five hundred! Mercy!"

Henry chuckled and made a gesture with his arm that he hoped was not awkward. "Wouldn't you like to sit down?"

"Sure." Marian promptly seated herself on the steps and made room for Henry beside her. "Since there is nothing I can add to your list of worldly dissipations we might consider another angle of human enterprise and endeavor." She looked at him with apparent flippancy and yet, far away and showing faintly, there was a fresh light in her gray-blue eyes. "I was referring to the matter of love-making. Did your father teach you how to make love? Or did he have some books on it in his library?"

All Henry's composure vanished again. He drew in his breath as if he were about to do hard work and said, "No."

"Then I'll be useful after all," she said gallantly. "I'll teach you how to make love, Henry. Possibly you may not find me ideally suited to your own needs. Doubtless after I've wasted many valuable evenings coaching you, it will turn out that you prefer brunettes. But I'm a girl of spirit. A stranger in a strange city deserves consideration. When would you like your lessons? Say, Mondays, Wednesdays, and Fridays from nine to twelve-thirty with options on the next three hours? We'll begin with hand-holding, dinner-table flirtations, winking, nudging, foot-foot and progress from there to embraces, kissing, vehement phrases— " She stopped because she had just looked at Henry. On his face was an expression of amazement and shock.

For a moment she was silent. Then, quickly, she took his hand. "I'm sorry, Henry. I didn't mean to do anything like this to you. I was just kidding. Teasing."

He looked at her then, turning his head slowly, and he spoke in a deep, dull voice. "It is I who must apologize. I have no idea under these circumstances of what I should do. I didn't know that ladies talked about things like that as you have just been talking about them. And if— I mean, since— they do, I don't know how to respond."

Marian nodded and relinquished his hand, which dropped inertly on the stair carpet. "I probably just wanted to find out what you'd do. You're pretty nice, Henry. I've never in this city, or any other, met two hundred and twenty pounds of absolute purity and punctiliousness before. The playboys up and down the avenues of this little hometown of mine are decadent at fourteen. Look. I'll try to teach you what you ought to know without being mean to you. But first we've got to see the sights. I made grandfather promise to take me along. Do you mind?"

He stood up. "Not if you can further tolerate the society of a fool."

"It's called the Empire State Building." Elihu Whitney leaned forward and spoke to his chauffeur. "Just pull over to the curb a moment, Gedney."

Henry looked. His eyes traveled to the cylindrical, shimmering apex of the colossal obelisk, and then back to the street. He watched the ant-swarm on the pavement as if he were wondering from what incredible source they drew sufficient courage to walk beneath these awful structures. He stared again at the surrounding buildings, dwarfed by the Empire State Tower. Blue sky and sunlight seemed phenomena subsidiary to this man-made thing. Perception of such magnitude made him ache. It was a shock to bring back his eyes to the old man and the girl who sat beside him in the tonneau of the car. They were still novelties — but in the confinement of an apartment they had seemed more like what Henry had expected people would be, than they did here on Fifth Avenue.

They were looking at him, waiting for him to speak. He tried to push the right words into his consciousness but they would not come. Instead, he looked again at the skyscraper beyond the place where its altitude was credible, beyond that to the place where his insular sense of proportion was shattered, and his eyes suddenly filled with tears.

He felt Elihu Whitney's arm around his shoulder. He heard

the old man's voice telling the chauffeur to drive on. He realized in the midst of his poignant muteness that the girl and her grandfather were exchanging a long, meaningful glance.

"Your New York offices."

Once again Henry found his eyes straining upward at the window-made geometry of unleashed, up-leaping surfaces.

This time he smiled. "Mine? I really have rather nice offices, haven't I? What floor are they on?"

Whitney chuckled. "Any floor you like. The whole building is yours."

"Very convenient."

"And another building just as big in Chicago," Marian said, looking at him, "and another in Seattle, and another in San Francisco, and one in Pittsburgh. Oh, you have lots of buildings, Henry. You can play house in almost any city in the country without having to pay rent. Of course I hope you'll make your headquarters in New York. But then I'm just a little frivolous girl who'd be jealous of the equally frivolous girls in the other cities if you moved."

Whitney half interrupted his granddaughter. "Would you like to go in and meet Voorhees?"

"He's the man at the head of all father's papers, isn't he?"

"Your papers, my boy."

Henry considered. "He's the man who you say mismanages the estate? Goes in for cheap politics? Graft?"

"He's the man."

"I'm surprised, if what you say is true, that he was allowed to remain in such a powerful position."

The car had stopped at the curb near the doors of the Record Building. Elihu Whitney glanced at the young man beside him. There was fire in his eyes when he spoke, yet he kept turning his gaze toward the tremendous bronze doors as if he expected an eavesdropper to come out of them. "You're the only man in the world who can interfere with Voorhees, son. Let me repeat, I've been waiting for the day of reckoning that would be represented by your return— or your father's— for a whole generation and more. I was powerless, legally, to change anything so long as the Stone newspapers made money. But I've watched in silent fury, and with an aching heart, the perversion of the finest newspaper reputation in the world to a reputation for scandalous, brazen, unprincipled, thieving, lying, blackmailing, rabble-raising villainy. I've watched Voorhees become one of the most powerful men in the country, an elector of innumerable foul politicians, a salesman of bad securities, a giant public grafter, a scourge, and a menace."

"You mustn't get so excited, grandfather." Marian addressed the old man, but her eyes were on Henry.

Whitney shrugged. "I can't help it. What do you say, Stone? Shall we go up?"

Henry had no criterion for measuring sinister men. He had expected someone ugly in appearance and uncouth in behavior. But he saw, seated behind a magnificent desk in a vast, cool, tasteful, and altogether peaceful-seeming office, a man of perhaps fifty with curly iron-gray hair, bright, straightforward eyes— eyes that a more experienced person might have found too candid— with an urbane smile and an outstretched hand. He found a man, elegantly dressed, whose diction was impeccable, whose voice was cultured— a man with none of the seeming of the rascal.

Whitney took Voorhees's hand and smiled at his words of greeting: "Elihu! Delighted to see you. It's been a long time. And you, too, Marian." He looked then inquiringly at Henry.

The old lawyer allowed his inspection to continue for a fraction of a second, during which Voorhees's face was subtly altered.

Then Whitney laughed, apparently in completely good humor. "I see you're beginning to guess my little surprise. And you're correct. This is Henry Stone."

Once again the newspaper publisher's face betokened a

slight, but definite, variation. He strode around his desk and seized Henry's hand in both of his. "Stone! Good God, young man, what a surprise! And what a story!" He smiled ruefully, then. "And how we've mishandled it. We've made the young scion of our founder into a Tarzan, without any real information about him at all."

Henry, in the suit that Elihu Whitney had secured, with his absurd mustache shaved away, was certainly spectacular, but he made a picture far removed from the stone age. He was different from other men only because of his superb physique, his indelible tan, and his immaculate eyes. He answered Voorhees embarrassedly.

"I'm very glad to make your acquaintance. I don't think the reports of me that I have seen in the *Record* did my pride any permanent injury. But they did serve to add to my confusion."

The confidence of Henry's speech discomfited Voorhees. He glanced at Whitney, who said archly, "You see he will be quite able to look out for himself in this newfound world. Even, I dare say, to look after his possessions."

Voorhees surveyed Henry surreptitiously while he opened a desk drawer, took out a box of cigars, and passed them. He glanced thoughtfully at Whitney as the old man lighted his cigar and observed a smile behind the gnarled hands.

Finally Voorhees spoke, his voice casual and his words identifying themselves in the air as exhaled smoke. "You intend to follow your father's footsteps, Mr. Stone?"

Henry shook his head diffidently. "My father trained me in as much of the theory and practice of newspaper work as he knew."

Elihu Whitney interrupted him. "Going to be a rude awakening, eh, Voorhees? Back into our midst, unsullied and unchanged, come all the ideals, all the eagerness, all the public principles and ambitions of an older and a better day. They come with millions behind them and a score of great newspapers for a voice. For years and years I've wished I was young again. And a thousand times I've wondered what this boy's father would do about the cesspool modern life has become. Egad, we'll find out!"

Voorhees's brow had faintly darkened, but he wore an industriously mustered expression of amused agreement.

It was Henry who spoke, partly from common sense and partly because of the confusion into which he had been thrust: "If you gentlemen are counting on me for any such exhibition, you seriously overrate me."

Whitney glanced hastily at him and so did Marian. "Of course we don't expect you to set the world to rights in a day— "

Henry nodded. "Or perhaps never. You see I don't know anything about the world. I'm just beginning to realize that what my father taught me about newspapers will be useless to me. It isn't my world or my responsibility. The sort of verbal fencing to which you have just resorted is not in accordance with my nature. If subtleties of this sort must exist, they will do so without me." He paused. "I see I have offended both of you, but I might as well make my position clear now as later."

Elihu Whitney broke through Henry's words with an anxious phrase: "Don't you think you better reserve all your opinions until later?"

Henry shook his head. "I hate to be disappointing, but I've seen enough of newspapers to know that I'm an ignoramus where they are concerned. My father taught me to make decisions for myself and to make them quickly. I shall certainly spend a year, and possibly two or three, in the mere business of acclimating myself with this new and fantastic world." He smiled a little. "You, Mr. Whitney, in your eagerness to see certain ideas of your own materialize, and you, Mr. Voorhees, in your natural agitation about your future status in my concern, have both overlooked the fact that I have been in the most solitary sort of confinement and isolation all the long years of my life. To put any sort of responsibility on my shoulders, to expect me to assume any such responsibilities, is unthinkable. It is obvious that I shall be compelled, whether I like it or not, to leave everything in status quo for a very long time. Have I made myself clear?"

To that long and careful speech there were three reactions. Elihu Whitney threw away his fresh cigar and grunted. Marian stared through the high windows at the skyline of New York, her lips pursed, her eyes amused and speculative. Voorhees rushed forward and took Henry's hand. "By George, young man, your judgment is as sound as your father's is reputed to have been, and I shan't forget the meaning of this expression of your confidence in me."

"This is Broadway," Marian said. She seemed to be talking with an effort, and its cause lay, at least partly, in the fact that her grandfather had not spoken a word since they had left the Record Tower. She glanced at him and went on conscientiously: "Street of fame and fortune, sin and sorrow. The Great White Way. The part we're going through now is Times Square. That triangular building is the Times Building. One of your competitors. Over there is the Hotel Astor. The skyscraper with the globe on top is the Paramount Building. Maybe tonight we'll take you to the movies. It's ten to one those two bleached-blond girls walking side by side over there do a sister act in vaudeville. And that man in the light tan trousers with the pink cheeks and the bright necktie— well— never mind about him. Don't sulk so, grandfather. What Henry said is perfectly true. It's as silly for you to expect him to launch all your ideas of reform in two hours as it is for him to pilot the *Graf Zeppelin* across the Atlantic."

Whitney did not even turn his head.

Henry glanced at the girl and then at the man and seemed almost to draw into himself physically as he did so. Finally he said in a deep and carefully measured voice, lifting it above traffic and keeping his eyes straight ahead: "You must admit that my moral obligation toward the world is debatable. You both would sympathize with my private reactions if you had spent as long a time as I have in so circumscribed a place. It is doubtless hard for you to realize that every one of these myriad people on the street is a new experience, a new interest, a profound surprise to me. For the rest — I'm afraid I must continue to seem ungrateful for your hospitality, and overproud."

Elihu Whitney stirred angrily and thumped on the floor of the car with his foot. "Bosh! I can remember when I was a young fellow. I used to talk that way myself. Your stilted logic. Your damn impertinent self-assurance. I've thought of your homecoming as a great draft of fresh air but it's only a bad memory. Look at all these people, then, since you're so eager to see people. Their mouths are turned down. They are sick, dejected, weary, wretched, cheated. Their birthright has been stolen by profiteers — by men like Voorhees. You could be their champion but since you prefer to be a little brass Gulliver, living on your newspaper's dirty money, why, go ahead, young man. The world is certainly your oyster. That I can't dispute." Again he stamped the floor.

Henry turned hotly and directly toward him. "I'd rather not discuss my future any further. I was impressed by Voorhees. He is a competent man, I am sure."

Whitney made a disparaging sound in his throat. "He's too damn competent. He frightened you, didn't he? That building and its elaborate contents frightened you, didn't they?"

Henry did not answer.

After some time Marian said: "I now wish to point out, dismally, that we are arriving in Central Park. It has miles and miles of paved roads and many fine trees, and flowers. A reservoir, bridle paths, and a zoo — "

Marian came into the library, where her grandfather sat moodily unoccupied in a huge chair. "Luncheon is ready."

"Where is Stone?"

"He's upstairs in his room. I've sent for him."

The aged lawyer stood up and walked back and forth across the room. "He's a misfit! A social anomaly! A popinjay!"

"He's been here less than twenty-four hours you must remember."

"He's made his attitude clear. He's afraid."

"Of what?"

Elihu Whitney snorted. "Of everything."

Marian shook her head. "I don't think he's afraid of what you think he's afraid of. Did you notice him as we drove around this morning? He was excited by the skyscrapers. He listened very intelligently to everything that was told him down at the Stock Exchange. He enjoyed the tour of the Record Building. But what he was really looking at all those hours, whenever he had any sort of a chance at all, was women — all women, old and young, beautiful and ugly. That's what he's thinking about. That's what concerns him. Everything else he said was just a sort of irritated desire to postpone the responsibility of being Henry Stone until he had in some way made up the interesting half of his biological life."

Whitney looked at his granddaughter. "By George, I wonder if you're right?"

She nodded.

He tugged at his beard and said, "In that case we should put his problems behind him as quickly as possible because I've got to see that boy do things in this world. With all the power he has — who's going to do it? You?" He stepped up to his granddaughter and tilted her head back so that her shining hair fell away from her eyes. "You'd like to, wouldn't you? But you'd have to remember that he's been trained by his father for thirty years and more to hate women, and to distrust them. He didn't act as though he had any emotions today, but I have a feeling that somewhere inside him there is a considerable fire burning, and it might not be the kind of fire that can be played with successfully. Then— consider yourself and him. It will certainly be a shock to him to find out that there is here and there a grain of truth in your checkered reputation. You're like all the girls of today. You look so angelic. And yet I imagine you could frighten a great many young men in a very few minutes— young men far more sophisticated than our impeccable islander. Still— if you're right— we may find him married to the first little doxy who is kind to him. There is that to think of."

Marian raised her eyebrows. "Has it occurred to you that this is very strange counsel for a grandfather to give his grand-daughter?"

The old man shrugged. "It has occurred to me that this advice is redundant and tardy and it has occurred to me that I, myself, have changed greatly since the seventies and eighties."

Henry opened the library door. His face was so impassive that discomfort was almost unreadable there. A few moments later they were summoned to luncheon.

Elihu Whitney sipped his coffee. Once again they had been spellbound while Henry talked about the island, although he discussed it with less enthusiasm than he had on the previous night and with some show of polite accommodation.

They were interrupted by a servant, who handed a note to Marian. She read it and passed it to her grandfather. "It's a young man named Tom Collins. He wants to see you."

Whitney scanned the note. "Collins? Collins? Tom Collins? Asinine name. Who is he?"

"He's a newspaper reporter," Marian answered. "He brought

me home from Webster Hall one night after Billy Laforge, who had taken me there, had passed out. He's a nice boy and if he wants to talk to you, you'd better go and see him. He works for the *Record*."

Whitney left the dining room and walked into the library. A young man rose as he entered. He was tall and angular, bright-eyed and cheerful-voiced. He had a wide sensitive mouth, a long sharp nose. His clothes were faintly collegiate, his bearing quick and informal, like that of many of New York's innumerable clever young men.

In answer to Whitney's, "Well?" he said, "I'm Tom Collins. I've been a reporter on the *Record* for the last three years. I resigned today because I was up here this morning with all the mugs who interviewed Henry Stone and I didn't write the story about Stone that Voorhees wanted me to write. It occurred to me, as I walked brooding and jobless along the city pavements an hour ago, that Stone might be able to use somebody like me. He's new here. I'm not. I can take a duchess to dinner at the Ritz, or chase a child murderer through the Mott Street dives. I'm a stenographer and a good two-fisted drinker, and I have an idea that I'd be useful in all those capacities. Besides, if Stone is going to manage his publications at all he'll find me a complete index of who's who and what's what, of office politics and political chicanery. I liked his looks this morning and I didn't like the run-around his own papers were giving him. They are afraid of him. I also came up here, Mr. Whitney, to tell you privately that I know for a fact that if Stone interferes too much with Voorhees and Voorhees's gang there's nothing surer in the world than that he'll be taken for a ride. I mean just that. Put on the spot. Bumped off."

A smile came and went on the face of the old lawyer. He sat down and lighted a cigar. "You seem to know a great deal, Mr. — "

"Collins. Tom Collins."

"Damned funny name."

"It was my father's worst habit."

Whitney nodded. "It might not be a bad idea. You'll have to see Stone himself, of course. He has taken his life pretty much into his own hands. He's difficult. By the way, just how am I to know that Voorhees didn't send you here?"

"Marian will give me a passport. We were like that about two hours once." Collins grinned. "I shall remember them as the happiest two hours of my life. Seriously, though, Mr. Whitney, this bird Stone looks like the goods to me. He could be a big shot — "

Whitney rose. "Perhaps so. You tell him about it. I told him, and he seemed to prefer the idea of roller-skating, or throwing cards into a hat. I'll send him in."

"Anyway put in a word for me. Understand I don't need this kind of job so much as I want it."

Henry Stone shook hands with the young New Yorker very formally and said, "Mr. Whitney has just suggested that I hire you as a sort of personal assistant and general attaché. He has given you the very highest recommendation."

Tom Collins smiled cheerfully. "I told him what to say." He sat down on the corner of a table and swung one leg while he talked. "Listen, Stone, no matter what you do or where you go for the next weeks, and maybe months, you're going to be a target for the curiosity boys and girls. You could stampede any theater in town by appearing there tonight. If you will look at the afternoon papers, which will be floating through the streets in an hour or so, you'll see that some of them still hold to the idea that you're a sort of hairy ape, and others maintain that doomsday has been sounded for the wicked old Stone Publications by the return of the founder's son. Every paper has you in wrong anyway. It's my opinion that you're in a tough spot in every department of the game, and because I've knocked around this town long enough to know it too well, I thought I'd barge up here and offer my services."

Henry felt a considerable liking for this young man but, as in the case of Marian and her grandfather, he had no means of articulating his sentiment. He was unhappily compelled to adhere to the rigid social disciplines of his father. "I shall be very glad to make a trial of your services, Mr. Collins, and I appreciate their proffer."

Collins hopped from the table and said: "You better call me Tom and the first thing we better do is to go out to a speakeasy this afternoon and have a few hookers together so that we can get each other straight."

Marian, her father, and her grandfather were once again waiting in the library. It was dark outside and in the vertical valleys winked the red and green jewels that guided traffic.

For the third time Marian spoke to the butler: "We'll wait just a little longer."

"That Collins probably got him drunk," Whitney said.

"I hope he did," Marian answered.

Sidney Whitney looked at his father and his daughter and chuckled: "From what you say, we've caught a Tartar. Here he is. Nobody else in New York City would ring a doorbell so politely."

Henry walked into the room and spoke to them gravely. His eyes rested on each one as if he were seeing them in a new perspective. He made his apology for being late. "I am extremely sorry. I had no idea it was nine o'clock until Tom— that is to say, Mr. Collins— reminded me of the hour."

"Perfectly all right, Henry," Whitney said. "We hoped you were getting drunk, but apparently not."

"No. My father was very insistent on that point."

Marian rose. "Let's have dinner now, anyway. What have you and Mr. Collins been doing? You seem more frigid than ever."

Henry waited until they were seated at the dining table, then he said, "I have simply spent the whole afternoon listening to Mr. Collins. If a tenth of what he said is true— and he was able to demonstrate the truth of it— then these United

States have fallen on such times as are intolerable — at least to me."

Elihu Whitney's sudden tide of delight was checked by Henry's next words. "I have listened to accounts of scandals reaching even to the White House. I have listened to the whole story of that infamous man, Capone. And I was disgusted by every syllable of it. I have heard a great deal about the management and politics of our great cities and I have concluded that the less I traffic with this compound of greed and villainy the happier I shall most certainly be. Tomorrow I shall relieve you of my presence and take chambers somewhere in town until I find the most ideal way of avoiding and forgetting this scrofulous civilization." He looked first at the older Whitney and then at Marian's father. His eyes were furious, haughty, and disgusted.

"Gentlemen — I can scarcely see how that word can have meaning any more — if resistance to all this corruption and degradation is impossible, then I am not sure that I, myself, would choose to live in the midst of it all."

For a moment Henry was possessed by a frantic excitement. Then, suddenly, bitterly he flung down his napkin and stalked from the room.

"A damn quitter. God, how mawkish and self-righteous we must have been forty years ago, Sid." Elihu Whitney almost shuddered.

Two hours later Henry stood looking over the light-studded silhouettes of Manhattan. He had left Tom Collins in almost the identical manner he had left the dinner table. All his father's teachings, had he known it, had been perverted and warped by a desire to make his son a perfect man seeking perfection. Their total effect, as it was exerted now, however, in the face of realities of a semi-civilized world, was merely revolution and despair. Henry did not understand himself. He did not understand especially that the wild and arbitrary boiling of his emotions was partly a psychological escape from other emotions that had been stillborn on the island, awakened faintly when Marian first came into the room on the night before, and that were now burning secretly and feverishly underneath his synthetic and yet passionately supported exterior.

When there was a knock on his door he whirled away from the window, yanked his fists out of his pockets, and clamped his lips together.

The knock was repeated.

He stalked to the door and pulled it open.

Outside Marian stood. She was dressed in blue-green satin pajamas that clothed her in liquid lines and that made a kindred background to her soft upturned eyes.

"I was sitting in my room for a long time," she said, "and the idea of having you here in the apartment, hungry and unhappy, was unendurable. So I came down. I wanted to talk to you, Henry."

He felt hollow and weak and small. He backed away from the door. She came in and closed it.

"Sit down," she said. She found a box of cigarettes on a table, handed one to him, and bent forward while he held a match. "You know, Henry, you're not just being a spoiled child because the world isn't heaven."

"If you wish to call an attitude of outrage and disdain being a spoiled child — "

She shook her head. "No, Henry. Although I must say those are the two principal results of being spoiled. It's something else. All this internal tumult of yours is real enough, I know. But by taking it out on poor grandfather and on Tom Collins you're just kidding and confusing yourself."

"I'd rather be left to my own opinions concerning myself."

"You always have been, haven't you, Henry? So how can you know whether they're right or wrong? Now you stay right in that chair and listen to me. I know what's the matter with you. You're frightened. People never get mad and act the way you do unless they're frightened. But you're not frightened by the world's perfidy." She locked her hands behind her head and caressed her temples with the inside of her arms. "You're afraid of me, Henry."

"Am I?" His voice was sullen and retreating.

"You've been kept from being a man— from seeing a woman — for so long, Henry, that all your frustrations are crystallized into one dreadful fear. Not only of me, but of all women. You behaved badly today just out of primitive, simple spite. All this furor of yours is nothing but sour grapes." She looked at him intently. "Aren't you afraid of me, Henry, right now?"

He returned her gaze. Once again he was seized by the same formidable contraction of his body and soul that had spellbound him on the previous night when Marian walked into the room. He could not move or speak. He scarcely breathed. His ears roared and a welter of intolerable pain surged through him and concentrated itself in his throat. Suddenly, and unwantedly, two tears gathered in his eyes and coursed down his cheeks. The proudest man in all the world, the man most open to its unkind cuts, began to cry.

In a moment he learned one sweet use of woman.

Marian went to where he sat with his head bowed. She put her arms slowly around his tremendous shoulders. She insinuated the liquid satin of her dress and herself into his lap. She kissed him slowly on the mouth.

A moment passed. The tornado in Henry Stone broke its chain.

A longer time, much longer, and even for Marian a very strange time, went by before a temporary end was put to the delirium in his eyes.

Then afterward, sitting in the same chair, smoking another cigarette, looking at him quietly she said: "Poor Henry! Poor, poor Henry!"

He shuddered. There were upon his face a thousand signs of things half remembered, a thousand incredulities. She watched him struggle back to something he could never be again, to something he now tried to be with the most profound absurdity of all his many absurdities.

"I'm sorry. I'm ashamed. Of course I shall marry you as early as possible tomorrow."

The cigarette fell from her fingers and she picked it up. She wanted to laugh. She wanted to scream. She very nearly wept. Then she was angry. She countered this towering asininity with a single sentence: "My dear Henry, I've loved so many men that it would be impossible to marry them all, and whether or not I could arrange it with you depends on what you do in the future."

For one clock-tick he looked at her, as baffled and as bewildered as the sudden materialization of a grotesque apparition might have made him. He saw her anger. He saw that she had told the truth.

She kept him from plunging headlong through the window only by screaming so loudly that he was once again stripped of the power to act.

At nine o'clock on the next morning the telephone in Henry's hotel suite rang dispassionately. Since midnight he had been walking back and forth in that hotel room, ingesting bit by bit the ingredients of his shame and remembering hour by hour each syllable of his father's hideously accurate diagnosis of womankind.

He stopped his endless marching and picked up the telephone. He believed that he was all dead but life stirred somewhere in him when he heard McCobb's voice.

"Hello, lad. I tried to get you at Whitney's house. What happened over there? They spoke of you very strangely. I wanted to ask you if all was well with you and how you like the new world."

Henry picked random words. "Well enough."

"I've been reading the tripe they publish about you in the newspapers," McCobb continued. "It's a strange land we've returned to. I'd be lost myself, but a cousin of my wife's has come forward with a home in New Jersey. She's a dour little woman, being Scotch, and it was my money she heard of first, but she's taken me in."

"Is that so? I was meaning to see you." Henry's voice was toneless.

"Don't bother about me, lad. For an old man, I'm doing grand. They found all the little things I made of gold and they've started saying I'm a great artist. They're giving me an exhibition, mind you, and they've promised me another fortune besides the handsome sum your father left to me. I have to keep my feet off my wife's cousin's chairs and I'm not allowed to give presents to her bairns, or spill my pipe on the floor, but it's a rare treat to be taken in."

"Have you seen Jack?"

"I have that. He's the king of Harlem, I understand. They treat him like a lord and he bought today a yellow automobile and a purple suit."

Henry almost laughed. "I'll see you both as soon as I'm straightened out about things."

"You can do it, being young. To me— it's a mad world. Well— good night to ye, lad."

"Good night, McCobb. And God bless you."

"Thank you."

Henry hung up. The sound of McCobb's voice had conjured up memories— memories of a lazy blue bay and a quiet house, of warm sun and hard work. Of untarnished fun, real hunger, and deep sleep.

A world without unease. A world without women and the strange emotions and acts to which they gave rise. Henry could hear Jack's dinner gong banging and McCobb's cheerful whistle. He bowed his head on the vast book that held old newspapers.

Henry had been in New York for a month.

He sat in his rooms in the Hotel Boulevard and thought about that month.

The expression on his face was melancholy and confounded. He stretched in a chair and smoked a cigarette.

His retrospect always began with Marian. He could not pry his imagination away from the paradox she presented — an aspect of freshness and candor worn over a disillusioned and betrayed heart. He thought of her in those terms. Every fact that emerged from his contact with her had served to fortify and embellish the definition of womankind that his father had pounded into him.

Being a gentleman, he had not violated the confidence imposed upon him by her anger. He had merely gone to Elihu Whitney that night and said that he could not presume on his hospitality any longer — that he felt he would be freer to do his work if he had his own establishment.

Whitney had guessed the source of Henry's sudden change of his plans. He had accepted it only after much protest, and with a feeling of wretchedness.

He was old enough to know the futility of interfering with the quarrels of the young.

Henry had moved — hating himself for moving, dreaming secretly that Marian would at least ask him not to go, and piqued by the fact that she failed to appear at all.

His mind traveled away from Marian only when it became fatigued with following the same closed circuit of thought. The rest of the month had been strange and often — despite his unhappiness — exciting.

He had flown over New York. He had learned to drive a car.

He had read twenty books about modern life — some technical, some speculative. He had seen the subways and the railroad stations, power houses, bridges, factories, steel mills, the departments of the municipal government, schools, theaters, a passenger steamship, a zeppelin, the interior of his newspaper plant, a modern hospital, laboratories, a dozen office buildings, hotels, night clubs, docks, slums, the houses of half a dozen millionaires, speakeasies, department stores, clubs, country houses on Long Island, Coney Island, the New Jersey suburbs, the Stock Exchange — everything that Collins could think of that he should see and observe.

He had kept Collins, whom he had liked from the first hour of their meeting. Collins was two years his junior — but he sometimes seemed decades older than Henry.

By and large, Henry had not enjoyed what he saw. Everything was a reflection of his first impressions, colored by his father's lessons and marred by his experience with Marian. Anyone taken from the late nineteenth century and hurled into the present day without preparation would experience the same dismay and revulsion.

Those who lived through it witnessed a change so gradual that it seemed almost inappreciable — although thousands of the older generation are still perpetually raising their hands in horror. They saw the polka become ragtime and the ragtime war music and the war music jazz. They watched corsets disappear and skirts rise and rouge come slowly to the lips of the guileless. They were shocked by the flapper who drank from a flask until the flapper became so familiar that she was commonplace and until they perceived that the skies had not yet fallen.

Other things happened step by step to that generation. Prohibition came — and they assumed that their own drinking could continue and were resentful of any effort to check it. When rebellion became a fad, they marched in the van — and as that rebellion bred gangs and political corruption, they looked on calmly, because it was not they who felt they were to blame.

Meanwhile the newspapers, and the magazines, the cinema and the radio and thousands of novels broadened their attitude toward morality. Things were said in print that had not been put in writing since the silver age of Rome. There were mutterings and censorships, but the movement toward tolerance and frank examination rolled over them. Psychology developed a new sense of the reasons for human behavior that the public slowly and partially assimilated. Thirty years of education and change marked the twentieth century.

Henry had missed them all. He came untouched from the old era. His dilemma was not surprising.

Nevertheless, he learned. He read the books on psychology with feverish interest. His mind understood what they said, but his emotions rebelled against it. Training is, unfortunately, almost always stronger than logic.

When he thought of the net totals of his experiences during the kaleidoscopic month, he foundered. He distrusted the new world, rather than the world for which his father had prepared him. Sometimes he sat up until the night was spent, discussing it with Collins and, while their viewpoints were irreconcilable, they remained steady companions.

He was turning over the wealth of material he had garnered when Collins came into the room.

"Hello, Henry."

"Hello, Tom."

"Still trying to judge your peers?"

"Still trying."

"How about a snack of supper? I thought of three things you haven't eaten yet. Armenian pastry, doughnuts, and hot chocolate."

"Not hungry."

"Well— later. Did you see what Voorhees wrote about you in the late edition today?"

"No. He called me up, though."

"Oh? It may be true, then. He says that you have decided not to make any changes in the *Record* staff and to permit the same directorate to operate it."

"That's what I told him. Only — I said — just for the time being."

Collins nodded. "So I thought. But Voorhees forgot to mention that you said just for the present. Your Tom — meaning myself — didn't believe the decision was final. With all your febrile distaste for things as they are, you'll want to get in there personally and break a leg for old Righteousness one of these days."

"I'm not so sure."

Collins lighted a cigarette. "Let's see. That makes the three hundred and seventy-ninth time you've expressed that particular doubt. It's your next to favorite doubt. Your favorite doubt is relative to women. Your third favorite doubt — "

"Say!"

"I have already discarded the subject."

"It's a relief."

"Good. I've been about town. There's some nasty dirt on the subway situation. Something like three million dollars has turned up unaccounted for. But Tom knows. That three million — or, at least, one chunk of it — was spent on a girl named Phoebe — nice name — last winter at Miami and on the little horses that ran but not quite fast enough. Oh — I'm brimful of scandal today. They caught Toledo Scarsi last night red-handed and by that I mean with red hands and he was bailed out at dawn today for the immense sum of fifty dollars. You remember my telling you about Scarsi — the lad of baseball bat renown?"

"It all makes me sick."

"And I saw your girl friend."

Henry sat up abruptly. Then he relaxed and said, "Whom do you mean by that?"

Collins chuckled. "A little less speed on the uptake for what is known as feigning innocence. You shouldn't have jumped.

You should have flicked ashes from your cigarette— it would be fine if you wore a monocle, because then you could have screwed it into your eye— and you should have said in an absent-minded voice, 'Girl friend? Girl friend?' That, Henry, would have been first-class feigning. I saw her in a speakeasy and I have to report that she was tight."

"You mean— intoxicated?"

"As you so effectively put it— intoxicated. She was intoxicated and tearful. I think she misses you. I think she is sorry. If I were you, I'd shag over to their little cozy-home and— "

"Never mind. Intoxicated. It's bestial."

Collins was sorry he had told Henry. It was the truth. Marian had been drinking and she had also been crying— both for the same reason and Collins knew the reason.

"She's proud," Collins hazarded.

"She must be— to get drunk in a public place."

"A speakeasy, in spite of modern custom, is not a public— oh— hell, old man— I didn't mean to hurt your feelings."

"You didn't," Henry replied evenly. "But I would rather discuss something else."

"Very well. I'm trying to cheer you up. I reserved the best for the last. I have a surprise for you."

"Yes."

Collins crossed the room and opened the door. "Come in," he said.

Jack crossed the threshold. He was dressed in a plain blue suit and he carried a black suit case. His face was clouded with apprehension.

Henry sprang to his feet. "Jack!"

"This gentleman told me I could come in, Mr. Henry— I— "

Henry embraced him. He pounded his back. "Jack! Good Lord, I've missed you. Where have you been? Why haven't you come before?"

Jack sniffed and moved his mouth. "Well, it's a long story."

"Sit down."

Jack glanced anxiously at Collins and sat gingerly. His eyes shone and he rubbed his white head.

"I been in jail. Things aren't the way they was. I got the money your father left — but it just naturally evaporated. I was what they call a big shot for a while. Then I got in a argument in a cabaret with a couple of high-hat young bucks and I busted boff of them in the jaw. I got in jail for two weeks."

Henry looked at Collins. "Why didn't I hear of this?"

"I didn't know till yesterday. I got him out. He gave the wrong name."

"I didn't want people to think that a man who has been associated with you, Mr. Henry, would get put in jail."

"Oh."

"People are different now," Jack continued. "It's all money, money, money and dance, dance, dance and drink, drink, drink."

"You've noticed that?"

"Yes, boss."

"Don't you think at your age that drinking and dancing and fighting are a little bit undignified?"

"Yes, boss. But I been on the island so long that I guess I just about broke loose." Jack's face was pale with apology.

Suddenly Henry roared with laughter. It was the first time Collins had seen him in the throes of the gargantuan laughter that had been born in his youth on the island. Collins was dumbfounded. The corners of Jack's mouth turned up.

When Henry's laughter subsided, Collins said, "I asked Jack if he'd like to come back and work for you. As your personal servant or your butler."

Henry stared at his old companion.

"If you could find a place, Mr. Henry," Jack muttered. "Some little corner — "

"My God! Some little corner, Jack? Why — do you know what? You're in charge of this place right now. You're Henry Stone's butler and major-domo. You're going to have a room right here. Collins, call the desk and make arrangements. Tell them that Jack is to have the best. He's my man and he's my friend."

Collins went to the phone.

Jack turned his back on Henry and stared out of the windows over Central Park.

"What's the matter, Jack?" Henry said presently.

Jack shrugged. "Nuthin'. Nuthin's the matter. Just looking. Just looking at them trees. I'm all right. Now. Just looking."

At ten the next morning Jack answered the phone. "This is the suite of Mr. Henry Stone, Esquire."

"Hey!" Collins yelped. "That's the desk. They know whose suite it is and the 'esquire' is redundant."

Jack turned to Henry. "Mr. Whitney to see you."

"Have him come up."

Henry waited nervously for the lawyer. It was difficult for him to be natural — Whitney was a constant reminder of Marian, and Whitney's manner had changed since he had left the penthouse.

He came in good humoredly, however, and put his hat on a table. "Morning, Henry. Morning, Collins. Hot. But not devastating. You probably don't mind it, Henry. You'll mind the winters. Wait till it snows."

"I suppose so."

"A few things here." The old man opened a briefcase. "A signature or two needed — and I've been sitting around my apartment for so long doing nothing that I thought I'd come myself."

"I'm glad to see you."

"Eh? Yes. This will clean up the whole transfer. And by the way — how are the Stone papers?"

Henry walked to the window. "They're all right, I imagine."

"You don't go down much, I hear." A little of the lawyer's good humor had left his voice. "Too bad. You could have a lot of fun right now."

"Is that so?"

"Well — your father would have called it fun. Voorhees and his gang are backing the new bridge bonds. The issue is just about double the amount the thing will cost. I was talking yesterday to Andrew Davis, the steel man. The *Record*'s full of propaganda."

"Mr. Whitney," Henry said slowly. "I don't feel equipped to meddle. I never saw a bridge until a few weeks ago. And I've been over the books of the corporations. They tell the story that seems to interest everyone to the exclusion of everything else. Profit: seventeen million dollars last year, Mr. Whitney."

The old lawyer grunted. "You need the money, of course."

Henry did not answer. Collins filled an awkward interval. "We've been making up for his lost life by taking in the city. He hasn't had much time to do things."

"I'm sorry," Whitney said, then. "I suppose we all regarded you as a sort of prophet. A prophet returned from the wilderness. Or perhaps as the reincarnation of your father. He was a fighter! But we expected too much too soon. The experience of a return such as yours must be overpowering. I am beginning to agree with you."

"Why?" In that one syllable was a note of passion, but as Henry continued, his voice was level. "Why? I didn't make your world the way it is. I'm not responsible for it."

"No. But you came here with what we thought was pretty fine thirty and fifty years ago." A hundred wrinkles appeared over the white beard. "We old fellows have always had a sneaking desire to see that crusading spirit let loose again." He sighed. "It isn't to be. When you said the world had changed — you were right. Humanity's off on a new tangent."

"It is." Henry turned his back. Collins looked at Whitney and shrugged.

The venerable lawyer walked across the room and put his arm over Henry's shoulder. "Don't take it hard, son. I — I loved your father."

Henry did not melt.

"By the way— Marian's been wondering why you haven't called."

"Has she?" The voice of the man from the island was cold.

Whitney's arm dropped. He picked up his hat. "I'll leave these things for you to sign. You can mail them to me."

"Very well."

"Good day."

"Good-bye."

Henry flung himself into a chair. He gnawed his fist and finally picked up the telephone and called Voorhees.

"This is Henry Stone," he said in a flat voice.

"Oh! Yes, Mr. Stone." Unctuous.

"I understand that bridge bond issue is too big."

"Really? You have the wrong information, Mr. Stone. I have personally checked all estimates. I think it is minimal. The board may be compelled, even, to float a second issue."

"Well— I'm going to take a chance on my information. I want a change of policy on it. The *Record* will get an estimate from Andrew Davis. He'll give one, I believe. I want an editorial saying that the issue is too big— twice too big— and that the margin goes into the pockets of city officials."

"That would be difficult, Mr. Stone. The *Record* is body and soul behind the present administration."

"Quite so. But we'll disagree with this project."

"But— "

"Order, Voorhees."

"Right!" No unction now.

"I'll be damned!" Collins said, when Henry hung up. He was grinning from ear to ear. "That'll get you in trouble."

Henry nodded without spirit. "I know. I shouldn't have done it. But I couldn't stand having old Whitney think I had no— what do you call it?"

"Guts."

"No guts. Besides— I am beginning not to like Voorhees. He's a— a— "

"Fat slob?"

"Precisely."

Collins began to whistle. Henry had fired a gun — apathetically, but directly. There would be a nice profit for Voorhees in his campaign favoring the bond issue. When his new program appeared, he would have to stand for a good many unpleasant telephone calls and interviews. Perhaps he would disobey Stone.

chapter
FOURTEEN

On the following morning, Collins woke Henry. Collins's face was tense. He had a copy of the *Record* in his hand. Henry sat up in bed and yawned.

"Here it is," Collins said. "'Davis Calls Bridge Issue Too Large.' Right on the front page. The buck's all on Davis. And the editorial is pretty weak — 'A few persons believe that there is nest-feathering in the bridge bond issue — among them Andrew Davis, President of the Eagle Steel Company.' More in that tone."

"Let me see." Henry read the editorial and the news story. "Weak is right."

"But strong enough to hurt Voorhees."

"I suppose so. I wonder if that will satisfy Elihu Whitney?"

Collins scarcely noticed the remark. He spoke quickly: "I think — if you'll look again at the front page — you'll see Voorhees's revenge."

"Revenge?"

"Bottom of the page."

Henry's eye fell upon the item Collins indicated. "Another Speakeasy Raid," it said. "Miss Marian Whitney and Other Distinguished Patrons Taken to Lock-up."

"That's Voorhees's answer." Collins kept his face studiously averted.

"What do you mean?"

"He's found out — or he suspects — that you are interested in Marian Whitney — or, at least, loyal to her. So he had her followed and the speakeasy where she went raided."

There was a long silence. "Oh," Henry said at last. "That's it?"

"He doesn't like his plans to be meddled with."

"I see."

"What are you going to do about it?"

Henry surprised Collins. "Nothing. Why should I? She was there, wasn't she? She deserves the ignominy."

Collins sagged into a chair. "And what are you going to do about the bridge issue?"

"I've done all I'm going to do," Henry answered petulantly.

Collins lighted a cigarette. Jack's voice came from the next room. He was humming. He picked up the telephone and ordered Henry's breakfast.

Henry did not look at Collins. When he was in the middle of his morning meal, Jack entered the room. "Lady on the phone. Won't give any name."

"Hello!" Henry barked into the instrument beside his bed.

"This is Marian Whitney." His heart congealed at the sound of her voice. "Thanks for the public reprimand. From now on, I won't have any disappointments to drown." She hung up.

"What's the matter?" Collins picked up a glass of water and handed it to Henry, who had turned sheet-white.

Whitney walked slowly toward the huge French windows that overlooked the city. "I pity him," he said.

Collins smoked.

"He's a misfit. That's all."

"I guess you're right," Collins murmured.

"His father's training didn't add to his natural strength. It vitiated it."

"Yes."

"The answer is— that the man of eighteen-ninety-eight can't cope with modern life. He's too feebleminded. Too tied up with conventions we've discarded. His idealism is as much out of place as a Sunday-school lesson in a trench fight. The things remembered from the good old days are colored by time. We weren't any more noble then— just smugger and more self-assured."

"I think," Collins said slowly, "that I'll give up my job as

secretary. He doesn't need or want me any longer. He just sits
in his rooms and broods."

"Stay a month more."

"Well — "

"Here's Marian."

She came through the library doors. She took off her hat and the sun shone through her hair. She was pale and tired. "Hello, grandfather. Hello, Tom."

"Hello." Elihu Whitney smiled feebly. "We were talking about Henry."

"I thought so."

"Well?"

"Why the 'well'? What do you want me to say?"

Collins offered a cigarette, which she took. "Anything you can contribute to the caucus."

"Why do you think I can contribute anything at all?"

Elihu Whitney walked to her side and patted her head. "We aren't going to cross-question you, Marian. But — well — we feel pretty badly about him."

"Who doesn't?"

Collins rushed in where his senior had feared to tread. "You were crazy about him."

Marian bit her lip. "Why not admit it? I was. I was crazy about him for two days. With the big craziness. I'd have slept standing up and lived in an ashcan and earned his living with a mop — for two days. What girl wouldn't? Even girls like myself, who are able in their modest way to see a good many men and interest them.

"He was built the way they paint wrestlers and that rust-colored hair was curly. He had eyes that hit — like bullets. And all his silly pompousness was sweet — then. Until I found out it was all there was. Just paste. A fool. Not a diamond in the rough — but a ten-cent-store diamond."

"He's inhibited," Whitney admitted.

"Inhibited!" Marian laughed. "He's all the repressions they've ever found and some more. I wouldn't undertake to salvage him if I could have Midas's touch and the Fountain of Youth in my back yard. He's frigid and nasty-minded. He's a fool! He's weak and pompous and spineless!"

"Don't cry," Collins said caustically. "Tears are spilled most pleasantly on the pillow. Here. Have a big handkerchief. We were rough, child. But we were trying to find an out."

"Let me alone." Marian struggled to her feet. "Let me alone. Don't you think I have any feelings? Don't you think I've been worrying and wondering and hoping? Don't you think I've been getting up every morning at seven o'clock to get the *Record* and see if there's any sign of backbone in it or even a rotten little paragraph with Henry's name over it?

"Don't you think that when I read about the bridge fight and found out that the dirt about me was done by Voorhees, I could have cheered? And then— nothing more. They practically took it back the next day. And the bonds are on the market. Don't you think I care?"

Elihu Whitney looked at Collins and nodded toward the door. Marian caught the gesture and sniffled. "Don't go on my account, Tom."

"I have to slide along anyway. Appointment."

"Well— "

"Thank you for calling, Collins," the lawyer said. "I'm afraid we can do nothing."

Collins walked slowly to the hotel. He found Henry closeted with an alert, elderly man.

Henry was obviously changed. He jumped up when Collins came into the room.

"Mr. Collins, this is Mr. McCobb. You recognize the name?"

"I certainly do. I'm delighted."

McCobb shook hands and Collins was astonished at his grip. "I've just been having a little talk with Henry."

"Yes."

"He's different, Mr. Collins. The city doesn't seem to agree with him."

"He's been working hard."

Henry interrupted. "McCobb's been in Washington. He has arranged for the United States to claim Stone Island."

"That's fine," Collins said politely.

"Isn't it!" Henry smiled happily. "The State Department has agreed to do it. And the Dunson Line is going to stop there twice a year — on the Batavia-Good Hope Route."

"Well!"

"McCobb's going back!"

The Scotchman nodded and smiled. "I can't stand the town, Mr. Collins. Either I'm too old for it, or else I've missed too much in between. The noise keeps me awake and the people here irritate me. I go bumping along the sidewalk and I get vexed with everyone that touches me. So I decided to go back. I'm taking a ship of my own and about a hundred people."

Collins shook his head. "Going to colonize it, eh?"

"Just that. We'll work the gold mines and the ledges where we found the jewels. We'll develop those zebu-oxen into fine cattle."

"That's not all," Henry cut in. "Professor Adam Smythe of Harvard and his wife and Professor John Doyle of Yale are going to go with him."

"Fine!"

"You bet it's fine. They know more about old civilizations than any other two men alive. Good Lord, I'd love to go into my ruins with them. They wrote McCobb a letter about the work I did deciphering the language. They say the people must have come from Mu."

"Oh, yes," Collins said. He had a feeling of being out of place in the conversation. "Mu."

"It's another continent that sank. They think they'll find a clue to the whole rise of man on Stone Island."

"That's very interesting."

There was a little pause. McCobb looked fondly at Henry. "I can hardly wait. I don't feel old anymore. By God, if I go back there, Henry lad, I'll bet I live to be a hundred."

Henry laughed loudly. "A hundred and fifty, McCobb."

"It doesn't seem possible. Think — lad — "

"Old Mount McCobb sticking its rocky head out of the jungle — "

"Jack's Lake lying like a sapphire in the sun — "

"All snouty with crocodiles — "

"And those big birds flapping on the rocks — "

"The lathe going in the shop again — "

"And the storms that come with the monsoons — roaring over the bay, knocking the thatch off the roof, churning up the sea — "

"And the swimming net — "

"With shark fins sailing along outside — "

"And new goats. You'll have to name them Four-eyes and Little Joe, too — "

"I'm taking bees with me this time. And a tractor. We'll have a farm on the pampas back there. And a power plant that I'm going to hitch to the waterfall on the side of the mountain. Just think of the old stockade all strung with electric lights — and a big searchlight to bring the boats in!"

"Don't say any more, McCobb. I'm so homesick I can hardly stand it."

Collins dangled his arm over the side of his chair. The door slammed.

McCobb leaped to his feet. "Jack!"

"Mr. McCobb!"

The huge Negro and the diminutive Scotchman pumped each other's hands.

"Henry told me you were with him again."

"Yes, *sir*! Indeed I am. I'm the major-domo here."

"That's fine!"

"McCobb's going back to the island, Jack," Henry said. "He's taking a lot of people. To live."

"Is that so?" A far-away look came into the Negro's eyes. He chuckled and then was still. He shook his head. "Be just like going home, Mr. McCobb."

"Won't it, Jack?"

Henry laughed. "How'd you like to be cutting a zebu steak again, Jack? And planting seeds out there in the garden?"

"Boy!"

"Or catching one of those silver fish?"

"Boy-oh-boy. Remember the one that weighed a hundred and eighty-two pounds?"

McCobb nodded. "I can still hear the roar you let out when it struck, Jack."

"It's a grand place."

McCobb moved toward the door. "I've got to get along. I'm having lunch with a fellow who knows how to get gold out of quartz."

"Great!" Henry said.

"See you again before I go."

"When are you leaving?"

"In two or three weeks."

"I'll be down to see you off," Henry said. "And if there's anything I can do for you, let me know."

Everyone shook hands. McCobb left.

Henry sat in a chair, thinking. At last he spoke. "I can get him a radio set. A big sending set, with towers, so that he can keep in touch with everything."

"Mmmm," Collins murmured.

"And we can get the stories of what they find in the ruins for the *Record*."

The one-time reporter lifted his eyebrows in surprise.

The door opened again and McCobb reappeared. "I just wanted to say, Henry— that if you ever get sick of the city— come out and see us."

"You bet I will!"

chapter FIFTEEN

Henry was different after McCobb's visit. He moved through life with a vast abstraction. He made several trips to the ship McCobb had chartered for his voyage. He offered a dozen suggestions of great value for their equipment. He did not go to the Record Building at all.

Collins knew what was in his mind: Henry wanted to go back. But Collins held his peace.

A week passed.

The *Record* embarked upon a campaign for the election of Tim O'Donnell for Mayor. Henry was only dimly conscious of it until one night when he happened to be riding in the subway. He often rode underground— the novelty of the darkness and trains seemed to numb the struggling anxieties of his mind, and the faces of the people absorbed his interest.

Henry was standing in a vestibule with his back against the brake-wheel. Two men talked loudly almost under his chin. They were plain men, in threadbare clothes. Their collars were soiled and their shoulders stooped. Henry scarcely realized that he was overhearing their conversation.

"Well," one of the men said, "I suppose they'll railroad O'Donnell into office."

"Sure they will."

"It's a shame."

"It's hell. I didn't register. I got so sick of voting on the beaten side that I quit voting. What the hell, I say."

"That's the way I feel. Last time I went to vote, there was a guy standing inside the booth. He came to the machine with me. 'I'll show you how to set it,' he says. 'I know how,' I answers. 'Oh, no, you don't— not that way,' he says and when I try to change my ideas— or his ideas— he taps me in the ribs with his fist. There's a cop outside laughing at me. So I votes— against myself."

"It's a crime!"

"Sure it's a crime. Milk too high and all water. Rent a million miles in the air. The grocer tells me they're collecting from him every week. Jeest!"

"An' this O'Donnell. That Myra Milo is his girl. Goes everywhere with him— even where his wife is. It's a crime."

Henry's attention had increased with each word. When the train stopped, he walked slowly along the platform. He burned with dull anger. His paper was behind all that. O'Donnell was his candidate. He walked up the street. It was— a crime.

He did not want to do anything about it. He did not want to enter into the dispute and muck. It wasn't his world. The afternoon was hot and breathless. Not his world. His head ached. His back ached. His eyes burned. The faces of the two men— wan and weak— floated before his imagination. Let them rot in their own mess.

He went up in the elevator. Collins sat listlessly, in his shirt sleeves, reading a magazine.

"Hello," he said. "Been down to the boat?"

"Yes."

"What's new?"

"Nothing."

Henry removed his coat. Let them suffer. He didn't invent the public. He leaned back.

"He taps me in the ribs with his fist. There's a cop outside laughing at me."

Damnation.

Henry snatched the telephone.

Collins looked up. "What's the mission?"

"Get the *Record*. Mr. Stone calling Mr. Voorhees."

"Good afternoon, Mr. Stone. Delighted to hear your voice. Warm weather— "

Henry was tired. He wanted to make it short. "Listen, Voorhees. I don't like O'Donnell. He's out."

"I'm afraid I don't understand."

Henry sighed. "Oh— hell! Listen, then. I'm going to campaign for Yates. I'm sick of O'Donnell and his gang."

"That's impossible, Mr. Stone."

"It isn't impossible. It's possible that if you don't carry out my orders there'll be someone who will in your place. That's possible."

A note Henry had never heard came in Voorhees's voice.

"Mr. Stone, I've warned you against a break between you and myself. I trust that this is not really your true opinion."

Henry's cold and sullen vexation left him. He was sorry he had called. But pride and habit made him carry through. He spoke dispassionately. "I mean what I said, Mr. Voorhees. If the *Record* doesn't turn over tomorrow morning on the matter of the municipal administration, I'll come down and change editors myself. I'll find somebody else. That's all."

Henry hung up.

Collins leaped on a chair and cheered.

Jack ran in. "What's the matter?"

"Nothing," Henry said slowly. "Nothing." Then to Collins: "I did that because I was disgusted. I've decided to go back with McCobb."

"What!"

"But I thought I might as well make one gesture before I left."

"Going to quit, Stone?"

"Yes."

"After a start like that?"

"It was foolish. A waste of time. I was angry— that's all."

"I see." Collins walked around the room. His thoughts of the *Record* conquered him momentarily. "God! It'll be funny. People are rushing right now to Voorhees with their hair on end. Big shots. And Voorhees's gorillas will be biting their finger nails."

"His gorillas?"

"Sure. The bodyguard in his office and the tough guys he

keeps hanging around every department just to be sure nothing goes wrong. Every man in the pressroom is a thug— Voorhees's private army always ready with strong-arm stuff."

"I didn't know about them," Henry said. "Toughs in the office, eh? That's like him. Jack!"

"Yes, boss."

"You can begin packing my things. I'm going back to the island."

The Negro almost lost his balance. "Am I— do I— ?"

"You want to go with me, Jack?"

"Yes, boss— " Jack gulped. "I want to go."

"All right."

Collins shook his head. "You don't seem to be very happy— even about that."

"I'm not happy— about anything."

"Going to say good-bye to Marian and her grandfather?"

Henry did not answer.

He went to the bedroom window. Collins followed. Lights had been turned on in the deeper canyons. The sun was sinking over the blue Jersey hills. He was going. He had not known it until he spoke.

Home.

All this— would be gone.

He turned and faced Collins.

"I'm going," he repeated. "You wouldn't understand why. But— " He picked up his thoughts. "I came here like Christopher Columbus. The new world was ahead of me. I was bursting with love for it, ambition, ideals. I had yearned for it for twenty years— ever since I was a child. I had been taught that it was a glorious place where a man could do a man's work.

"What did I find? First— something so beautiful and breathtaking that I could not contain myself. The buildings and the machinery. We never imagined anything like it on the island. It seemed to me that humanity was at last reaching up toward the stars. That it had climbed out of the earth. I was ecstatic.

"Then I looked again. You have to look twice to see. The whole world is sour. Rotten. Despicable. It has emerged from the most terrible war of all time — a war that accomplished absolutely nothing. Blood in rivers in every direction and afterward — jealous piddling of little men. It's sickening.

"Once there was in this country a standard of morals and manners. That's gone. Vulgarity is everywhere. In the theaters and the radio and the newspapers. Nobody cares. Vicious men run through the streets with machine guns and shoot down children. Demagogues and morons and even criminals are elected political leaders. The bodies of government have become a shambles of cheap wit and expensive graft. My father warned me against women — and the women have sunk beneath the men. They're painted prostitutes — even the old ones. Decency has deserted the best homes. Everyone fights for money. Money! There's madness for it. Greed and exploitation. War and corruption. Stupidity and hatred."

Henry had pronounced his anathema in a steady, low voice. He drew a breath and continued: "You — Whitney — ask me to do something about it. You expect that I shall be able to change it — able and willing — just because I was brought up in a tradition that once was American — a tradition that is averse to countenancing murder, to admiring public assassinations, to abetting corruption, to breaking the law, to being cynical about rotten banks, to gambling with hard-won savings, to rampant and gaudy publicity for sex and fornication, to adultery and infidelity, to the practice of sending the impotent and the malicious to Congress, to subjugation to political trickery, to bribery, public theft, half-baked campaigns in the name of modernity and for the purpose of pornographic profit, to lies and cheating, to a vast, cosmic hypocrisy that should make the body of even a tenth-rate nation turn crimson from shame and fight for its internal freedom until decency had been restored or suicide had been committed."

Henry stopped.

For once, Collins was not superficial. He seemed, even, to be stirred by a form of anger. He stood and began to talk.

"That's not true and that's not fair. Or — rather — it's only partly true. It's one side. You haven't looked at the other and you don't seem to care to see it. I don't give a red-hot God-damn what you think — but I can't help speaking about what you've said.

"You're in a country that's full of a hundred kinds of peo-ple — and that's responsible for part of the confusion and crime. But you're in a country where the world is being changed every day. You're in a country where men for the first time since the dawn have the courage to question everything. Where re-ligion isn't being handed from father to son as an immutable set of laws but is being sifted for what's worthwhile. To do that takes nerve. You're in a country where the people have grown sick of the pretense of the fashionable morals you're praising, and maybe not all their experiments are successes, but at least they aren't afraid to try."

Collins's words fell like rolls on a drum. "There's contest here. And look at science. You're in a world where men have given their lives by the hundred in rotten little laboratories and foul clinics to do away with disease and make humanity healthy. The stars are being weighed and the atoms pulled apart. You talk about the war. Maybe it didn't make the world safe for democracy — but there are a million men and more who believed that it would and plenty who went out there and got their hearts torn out because they hoped it would. Of course, there's confusion. Of course, there's crime and vice. When hasn't there been? But there never were so many people who wanted to end it and who were ready to help end it and who get down on their intellectual hands and knees every night and pray to whatever gods they have for someone to come along and help them end it. This is daybreak. The Middle Ages didn't end with the Renaissance. They didn't end with the Industrial Revolution. They're ending now, and only now. Man's turned honest and admitted his sins and his motives.

That made hell to pay, and that was the only way back over the long track of human error — to a little human happiness and decency and peace and development. You — "

Collins did not finish.

The bell on the door of the suite rang and Jack answered it. Henry stared at Collins in astonishment. Collins sat down, exhausted.

In the next room, Jack opened the door and saw three men outside. They had guns in their hands. Jack had had experience with the world, and with men, and he knew death when he saw it in human eyes.

He knew it was intended for Henry.

He interposed his huge body. "What you all want?" he said steadily.

"Mr. Stone here?"

"He's — "

"One side."

A revolver was poked into Jack's ribs. But Jack did not budge. His right hand had reached under his coat. He brought out an enormous butcher knife.

"You go away," he said.

"Get back, nigger. You'll get hurt." Tense, hoarse words.

"Go away — "

The first man — a little man with a black mustache — tried to get around Jack.

Jack side-stepped to confront him. The man paled and fired.

Jack's eyes blinked once. His knife fell upon a little man, cleaving down through his shoulder to the heart. Then Jack pitched on his face.

The other two men exchanged a terrified glance and one said, "We better scram."

Henry leaped into the room.

"Jack! My God! Jack's been shot!"

The door shut at Jack's feet.

Collins leaped upon it and turned the lock.

Henry bent over Jack.

"Jack! Jack!"

Blood ran from the black coat. The aged eyes opened, and seemed to recognize Henry. Then light dwindled in them.

Henry looked up.

Collins was standing stiff at the side of the wall. "Get over here," he said. "They may shoot through the door."

"But— "

The reporter grabbed Henry by the lapels and pulled him away. "It's Voorhees! Voorhees and his gang. They knew you could change the policy of all the Stone papers. They believed you would. They sent someone for you. Jack must have refused to let them in."

"Voorhees?" he repeated, still not understanding.

"Voorhees. It was the only way. Get you and get you quick. I should have been looking out for it. It's my fault— "

"They killed Jack!"

Collins shook him. "You're God-damned right. And they would have killed you instead if he had let them in."

"Voorhees did that?"

"Yes. Yes. Yes! It was the last straw— What in hell are you doing?"

"I'm going to see Voorhees."

"Don't be a fool. Don't open that door. Don't you see? You haven't got anything on Voorhees!"

Henry stepped away from the wall. His eyes were lowered to the body of Jack. He whispered the name.

"Jack— Jack— Jack. They killed you. These human lice who run this city. They shot you— because you chose to be shot instead of me. They— "

"Take it easy, Stone," Collins said in a gentle voice.

The man from the island knelt beside the Negro and folded his two hands. His throat had contracted so that he could scarcely speak. He stared up at Collins. "I loved him— almost as I loved my father."

Slowly a change came over Henry. His sorrow was submerged in a different and hideous emotion. His face locked. His eyes became a conflagration.

His body grew tense— the great shoulders lifting and the mighty head thrusting itself forward. He shook; his fists clenched.

"That's right," he whispered again. "I haven't got anything on Voorhees. That's the way with everything these days. He'd go to trial and get off. I haven't proof. But I'm going to see Voorhees just the same!"

The last words were ended with a roar. He whirled and yanked the door open without turning the lock. The hall was empty except for a body. He rushed down it, Collins behind him. He stamped and swayed until an elevator came.

He hurled himself through the lobby and started down the street. He did not even think of taking a cab.

Henry stalked to the newspaper building. Hatless. Not panting.

He got into an elevator and stepped out on the floor where Voorhees's office was. A girl at a desk rose when he entered the outer room. He ignored her and crossed through the maze of desks. Collins was still on his heels.

He opened another door.

Voorhees was at his desk, talking over a telephone. Two large, lantern-jawed men sat in chairs at his side.

When Henry entered, Voorhees hung up, and stood.

"Mr. Stone!" He seemed to be frightened.

Henry smiled and sat down.

"Mr. Voorhees."

"You weren't announced — "

"No. I dropped in to speak about the matter of the O'Donnell campaign."

"Oh — yes. I wanted to tell you. I didn't change the morning run. I thought I could convince you that O'Donnell was our man."

Henry shook his head. "No. I prefer Yates."

Voorhees swelled and purpled. "I think I can convince you."

"No."

"These two gentlemen — "

Henry lifted his hand. "Sorry. You're through. And I'm having you tried for murder. Three of your men shot my Jack."

"The lousy nigger pulled a knife — " Voorhees clapped his hand to his mouth in terror at having given himself away.

Something happened to Henry. He came up to his feet, slowly. The motion was like the setting of a bow — a long even pull that generated tension. Voorhees's eyes stuck on his. "That's what I wanted to know," Henry said in a childlike voice.

He got one of the lantern-jawed men as he dove over the table. Fist on jaw. His hands went around Voorhees's throat. The third man reached for his gun and Collins hit him on the temple with an inkwell.

Voorhees had just time to scream.

A door opened. Henry saw a group of men sitting in the smoke-filled directors' room — the politicians who had come to confer with Voorhees over Henry's interference with their plans. He dropped Voorhees and went into that room. Collins, behind him, turned out the lights.

Awful sound came from the dark. Someone shouted, "Don't anybody shoot!"

No one shot.

Presently a man ran from the room and out the door. Then two more men. Then one crawled out. The hubbub diminished. Henry was last to come. Collins, at the door, switched on the light again. Henry had the arm of a chair in his hand and it was bloody. There were five men on the floor in the room where Henry had been.

People ran toward the office. Two more of Voorhees's gorillas came with guns. Henry plunged at them. A bullet tore through the flesh on his back.

For a minute he stood in the center of the room — a frightful spectacle. His chest rose and fell. His eyes were berserk. His coat had been ripped off. His trousers were torn. His shirt was crimson. There was a great welt on his head.

Collins shouted shrilly in the ear of a man beside him. "Get the reporters, Billy. Tell them Voorhees's mob is coming after Stone. This is Stone. Tell 'em to bring clubs."

"We'll go down," Henry bawled.

On the way, Collins grabbed a hysterical clerk and slapped him into sense. "Call Elihu Whitney. Tell him to come here at once. Tell him hell is loose. Get the police!"

Henry tore for the stairway. He bolted the five flights down to the presses. He howled at a man in overalls to turn off the lumbering giants. An immense silence filled the place.

"I'm Henry Stone!" The voice rolled through the vast chamber. "I'm looking for anybody who's Voorhees's man. Any of you baboons— "

Someone fired at him through one of the street doors and shouted, "Get him, McCorsk!"

There was a rush toward Henry. No one could hold him. No one could hit him hard enough even to attract his special attention. Collins went in with a machine wrench. Then the reporters Collins had summoned from the city room came down. They stood at the door— a dammed-up avalanche— for just an instant. They understood what was happening.

"Come on!" someone shouted. "Somebody get the cops. Stone's taking on the mob. Get in there and fight!"

The holocaust raged around the stilled presses. Individuals separated from the main mass and slipped back and forth on the bloody cement. The feud between the reporters and the *Record* gang now had a leader. Men reached for tools and hurled them. Men stole through alleys in the machinery with bulging eyes, and fists clenching wrenches.

In the thick of the tumult Henry roared and swung his fists. He was the equal of ten.

Into every blow went all the superb strength he had gained on the island— all the hatred he had for the rottenness of the city— all the heartbreak he had found there and the misery that was pent in his soul.

He was a Titan.

By and by the din diminished. Henry and McCorsk fought together in the center of the chamber. Some men ran away. Some men lay still and looked through bruised eyes. Some of them could not look, in those gory moments.

Collins went round the edge of the fight, weak and gasping, his wrench in a hand he could no longer lift.

McCorsk was a huge man. He had a waist like a hogshead

and fists like hammers. He fought silently. But Henry fought back bellowing defiance.

It was upon that scene that Elihu Whitney and Marian made their entrance.

The pressroom was a charnel place. The men in it were ghouls. And in their center, McCorsk and Henry plunged remorselessly and unhindered against each other.

Henry spit blood.

McCorsk hit his head.

Then Henry saw Marian. He felt the other man's arms around him. He pushed him away. The brutal, red face dangled in front of him. Henry leered at it. He remembered his fury dimly. McCorsk hit again. Marian screamed.

Henry felt stupidly weary of the fight. His antagonist picked up a hammer.

"Hit him!" Marian screamed. "Henry!"

He shook his head. McCorsk crouched and circled. Henry saw him plainly, then. His magnificent and almost naked body shot into the last blow. It turned McCorsk's face to jelly.

Henry slipped to the floor, gasped, quivered, stood up, thought painfully, and then raised his voice. He tried twice before he commanded his former bellow.

"I'm Henry Stone. I'm the boss of this place. How many reporters are here?"

A half dozen men came toward him, Collins pushing them.

Henry wiped his face and coughed. "Well— well— new policy. New management. Me. I'm going to run this God-damned business. No more gangs. No— no— everything. We're going for straight government." He rocked on his feet, sobbed, and roared, "You tell them, Collins. Collins is managing editor now. You tell them. Reform. Clean city. I'll show Voorhees and his four-legged, yellow-livered baboons how to run a paper."

His head cleared a little more— although his breath was almost gone. "As for you"— he yawped at Elihu Whitney and his granddaughter — "you're right. I'm no gentleman! I — I'm a savage!!!"

He pitched on his face.

Police filled the newspaper building. Reporters with bandages on their arms and heads were writing history into the story of the change of policy in the *Record* and the other twenty-one Stone newspapers.

Henry lay on the couch in the office that had belonged to Voorhees and from which Voorhees had been removed — unconscious. Marian moistened his face with antiseptic and cotton. He opened his eyes. For a minute, he stared.

"Lie still, dear," she said. "You're terribly beaten."

Henry's manners had returned. He lay still. He spoke. "I apologize, of course. It was bestial. But — you see — I don't belong to this world. I don't understand its etiquette or its customs very well. I got mad."

She laughed softly. "Yes. You did get a little bit mad."

"You shouldn't be here."

"I think I should."

"Why?"

"Because I love you."

"Oh." He closed his eyes. He realized that he should remember something his father had told him long ago — but he had a feeling that, whatever it was, it had been a mistake.

"Would you mind saying that again?"

"I love you."

Again, he was silent for some time. "I think I know what you mean — now," he said at last. "It's something that father never knew — never understood. Love. It's bigger than jealousy. It's — it means that you will always love me not exclusively, but best and most."

She did not answer.

"It means — "

She kissed his battered face.

"That. It means that," he said wonderingly. "It means that —
and so much more — "

"Lie still, Henry. Please — "

He lifted himself on his elbow. "I don't know what to say.
I — yes, I do — get me a stenographer! I've got to dictate an
editorial. You can help me!"

"But — "

"Say! I'm a newspaper man now. Get a stenographer — but
kiss me before you go and have another kiss ready when you
come back!"

In the Bison Frontiers of Imagination series

In the Days of the Comet
By H. G. Wells
Introduced by Ben Bova

The Last War: A World Set Free
By H. G. Wells
Introduced by Greg Bear

The Sleeper Awakes
By H. G. Wells
Introduced by J. Gregory Keyes
Afterword by
Gareth Davies-Morris

The War in the Air
By H. G. Wells
Introduced by Dave Duncan

The Disappearance
By Philip Wylie
Introduced by Robert Silverberg

Gladiator
By Philip Wylie
Introduced by Janny Wurts

The Savage Gentleman
By Philip Wylie
Introduced by Richard A. Lupoff

When Worlds Collide
By Philip Wylie and
Edwin Balmer
Introduced by John Varley

To order or obtain more
information on these or other
University of Nebraska Press
titles, visit www.nebraskapress
.unl.edu.